Stand-By Date

Definition: A friendly member of the opposite sex willing to act as loving date at nightmarishly couple-centered events such as weddings, reunions and office parties.

Requirements: Must be witty, intelligent, good-looking and able to play the role of infatuated lover.

Warning: Under no circumstances are Emergency Stand-By Dates to fall in love. Will result in extreme emotional confusion and heartache.

Dear Reader,

Ah, yes...weddings. Reunions. Office parties. All those events that are just made for couples, people who walk in two by two, holding hands, smiling into each other's eyes... You get the picture. But for those of us who are not only single but currently unattached, it's more like being the center of attention for all the wrong reasons. "What's *she* doing here all alone? What a shame she hasn't got a boyfriend." Of course, maybe it's not a shame at all. Maybe "she" just decided to stop kissing frogs and let the handsome prince come looking for her. But still, it might be nice to have company on those occasions, and that's where Samantha Carter's *The Emergency Stand-By Date* comes in. It provides a novel solution to the dilemma, not to mention a happy—if unexpected—ending for the couple in question.

And then there's *Wedding Daze*, a first novel from brand-new author Karen Templeton. She used to work in a bridal salon herself, so she knows her background firsthand. Meet Brianna Fairchild and discover how it feels to spend your days planning everyone else's fantasy weddings, with no hint of your own groom in sight. Until you meet Spencer Lockhart, a confirmed bachelor with "Mr. Right" written all over him. Now, how to get him making a few wedding plans of his own...?

Have fun, and don't forget to come back next month for two more wonderful books all about unexpectedly meeting—and marrying!—Mr. Right.

Yours,

Leslie Wainger
Senior Editor and Editorial Coordinator

> Please address questions and book requests to:
> Silhouette Reader Service
> U.S.: 3010 Walden Ave., P.O. Box 1325, Buffalo, NY 14269
> Canadian: P.O. Box 609, Fort Erie, Ont. L2A 5X3

SAMANTHA CARTER

The Emergency Stand-By Date

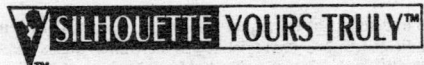

Published by Silhouette Books

America's Publisher of Contemporary Romance

If you purchased this book without a cover you should be aware that this book is stolen property. It was reported as "unsold and destroyed" to the publisher, and neither the author nor the publisher has received any payment for this "stripped book."

 SILHOUETTE BOOKS

ISBN 0-373-52063-8

THE EMERGENCY STAND-BY DATE

Copyright © 1998 by Shanna Swendson

All rights reserved. Except for use in any review, the reproduction or utilization of this work in whole or in part in any form by any electronic, mechanical or other means, now known or hereafter invented, including xerography, photocopying and recording, or in any information storage or retrieval system, is forbidden without the written permission of the editorial office, Silhouette Books, 300 East 42nd Street, New York, NY 10017 U.S.A.

All characters in this book have no existence outside the imagination of the author and have no relation whatsoever to anyone bearing the same name or names. They are not even distantly inspired by any individual known or unknown to the author, and all incidents are pure invention.

This edition published by arrangement with Harlequin Books S.A.

® and TM are trademarks of Harlequin Books S.A., used under license. Trademarks indicated with ® are registered in the United States Patent and Trademark Office, the Canadian Trade Marks Office and in other countries.

Printed in U.S.A.

Dear Reader,

I've been writing ever since I was a child, when I scribbled the stories I made up in my head into a notebook . It became a dream of mine to one day have a novel published, to go into a bookstore and see my book on the shelf. My dream took a more specific form when I was older and my mother shared her Silhouette romances with me. Then I wanted to write stories about love, to make readers laugh and cry with me. I began dreaming of one day having a novel like that published by Silhouette. With my previous Yours Truly title, *Dateless in Dallas*, I fulfilled that dream and saw my book in the bookstore.

Silhouette's Yours Truly line features the kinds of stories I most enjoy reading and writing: fun, contemporary stories about people finding love where they least expect it. As a writer and avid reader, I especially like the twist of having the written word play such an integral role in the story. I've often said that when I finally find Mr. Right, it's bound to have something to do with words in print, as much time as I spend buried in words—whether books, newspapers, magazines, letters or e-mail.

I hope you enjoy reading *The Emergency Stand-By Date* as much as I enjoyed writing it.

With warmest regards,

Samantha Carter

Books by Samantha Carter

Silhouette Yours Truly

Dateless in Dallas
The Emergency Stand-By Date

1

Normally, Ken Parks didn't believe in drowning his troubles, but this was one time in his life when he didn't want to be able to think coherently enough to analyze the decisions he'd made. He'd known the moment he saw Kristen walk down the aisle, a vision in white, that he had made the biggest mistake in his life. Feeling no need to inflict more pain on himself, he'd escaped as quickly as possible from the hotel ballroom where the wedding reception was held and staked out a seat in the hotel lobby lounge.

This was it, he vowed. He wasn't going to make any more big decisions by listening to his heart, which always managed to be wrong. Next time around, he wouldn't play the hopeless romantic. He'd be cautious and wait to see how the woman reacted before he decided to leap in headfirst. And he wouldn't give up so easily just because a relationship didn't meet all his idealistic expectations.

He looked across the top of his glass of rum and cola and noticed a woman cross the hotel lobby. When she turned to enter the lounge, he put down his glass and watched her. She was dressed for an evening out, wearing a blue dress that clung to gentle curves, then swirled around her thighs as she walked. Her light brown hair brushed her shoulders, and the overhead lights sparked hints of gold in it that shimmered as she moved. She held her chin tilted a bit too high, her spine a bit too straight. Her eyes were bright, as if they were about to spill over with tears. A paper name tag stuck to her dress declared that she was Jenny Forrest, a graduate of Jacksboro High School.

Ken turned his head when he thought he heard the lounge's band strike up a sultry number, but they were still on their break. It was probably the Muzak he'd heard.

Turning his attention back to the woman, he watched as she headed toward the bar. Maybe this evening wouldn't be a total waste. At the very least, she might be willing to listen to his sad story, and it looked as though she had one of her own to tell.

She slid onto the bar stool next to him, ripped the name tag from her dress, threw it in an ashtray and signaled to the bartender. She looked like someone about to go on a real bender. Good, Ken thought, glancing at the discarded name tag. He hated to drink alone, and he wouldn't mind "Jenny Forrest" joining him. It looked as if this evening was going to get much more interesting. Instead of wallowing in his own misery, he could hear someone else's sob story, and it was bound to be much more interesting than his.

The bartender approached and the woman said, "I'll have a glass of white zinfandel." Her voice was husky, with a slight Texas drawl.

Now Ken was really intrigued. White zinfandel wasn't usually the drink of choice for someone about to go on a bender. Either he was reading her body language wrong, or she had no idea how to go about drinking herself into oblivion.

She brushed her hair out of her eyes and took a deep breath, as though cleansing herself of a bad experience. Up close, he could see that her eyes were rimmed with red, although he didn't see any sign of tears on her cheeks. She was holding herself in control, but was very close to breaking down.

Ever the gentleman, Ken couldn't bear to watch a lady suffer without offering comfort. "Are you okay?" he asked, keeping just enough casual distance from her that she wouldn't think he was trying to pick her up.

She whirled as if he had just materialized on the stool next to her. "I beg your pardon?" she said, giving him an icy glare. The unshed tears made her eyes glow bright green. He was mesmerized, wondering if she used that glare to stun her prey, but he decided it was just the effects of a rum and Coke on top of several glasses of champagne from the wedding. He was far from drunk, but he wasn't thinking entirely rationally.

"I'm sorry," he said. "I didn't mean to intrude, but it may take you a while to get drunk on that stuff." He gestured at the pale pink liquid in her glass.

She arched an eyebrow at him. "What makes you think I want to get drunk? I'm having a glass of wine because that's what I want to drink."

He shook his head. "No, you didn't just happen to stop by this bar because you wanted a glass of wine. You might as well be wearing a sign that says I'm Having a Bad Day." He gestured toward her. "You're barely holding yourself together—but doing an admirable job of it," he hurried to add when her glare intensified. He gave her his most winning smile. "So, what's your story? Does it have something to do with that name tag you were so quick to get rid of?"

She shook her head and frowned. "Why would I want to share my story with you?"

Because I want to know all about you, he thought, although he wasn't really sure why. He nipped that thought in the bud, remembering his earlier vow to himself. Out loud he said, "Because the bartender seems to be ignoring us troubled souls. Come on, it will make you feel better to talk about it. We're like strangers sitting next to each other on an airplane. We can tell each other all our troubles, then we'll never see each other again. It's like therapy, only cheaper."

She worried her lower lip with her teeth, and one tear finally splashed over her lashes onto her cheek. She wiped it away with one hand, but the damp spot remained on her cheek, along with a tiny smear of eye makeup. "Oh, hell," she said in a shaking voice. "I swore they wouldn't make me cry."

"Who's they?" he asked, leaning closer and momentarily forgetting his own troubles.

She gave him a crooked smile. "Did you go to your high school's ten-year reunion?"

"Yeah."

She licked her lips and studied him for a second. "Let me guess. You were Mister Popular, class president, a jock. And now that you're grown-up and successful, everyone was even more impressed."

He shook his head. "You've got it all wrong," he said, then grinned and took another sip of his drink. "I was vice president."

"And I take it you're single," she said, indicating his bare left hand.

"Oh yeah, I'm single, that's for sure," he muttered, draining his glass. He really hadn't needed that reminder.

"And I bet no one thought anything of it. You probably had a date with you, anyway, someone attractive, maybe even someone you'd known back in school."

She was right there, too. He had taken Kristen. He hadn't dated her in high school, but her parents and his parents had been friends as long as he could remember, and he had known her then. "Yeah, I had a date."

She took a healthy swallow of wine and tossed her hair back. "Well, I wasn't popular. I went to a small school, and still no one knew who I was. I've improved a lot since then, and I hoped someone would notice. But all they noticed was that I came without a date. No matter how successful a woman is in business or anything else in life, the main measure of success is whether or not she's snagged a man." Her voice rose, and her cheeks grew flushed as she spoke about what was obviously an emotional issue for her.

"That's rough," Ken conceded, although he wasn't sure it compared to watching his life fall apart as the woman who was meant for him married his best friend—at the very moment he realized she was made for him.

Jenny Forrest swirled her wine around in her glass and said, "You know, it sounds kind of silly now that I think about it. Most of the time, I don't care that I don't have much in the way of a social life. I've got a great career, a few good friends and plenty of things to do. I don't need a man to make me feel complete. But a night like this makes me wish I had a good emergency stand-by date."

"Emergency stand-by date?" he asked.

She tilted her head to one side. "You know, a friend of the opposite sex you can take to office parties, weddings, class reunions—any time you need a date and don't have a significant other to bring."

"And how does one qualify to be an emergency stand-by date?"

"The first part is easy. They just have to be presentable in public and capable of behaving in a way that won't embarrass you. The second requirement is the tricky part. They have to be aware that they're just doing you a favor as a friend, one that you'll return. Your asking them to go to these events with you is not an indication of deep, undying passion and should not be construed as a romantic overture."

"So, basically a safe date—a friend."

She nodded. "Exactly."

"And you don't have a handy emergency stand-by?"

She sighed and wilted a little. "No. No one," she said, shaking her head. "Co-workers aren't safe—and besides, I didn't want them to get any ammunition from meeting my high-school classmates. And I don't know anyone else right now, not that I'd want to bring with me to something like this."

He studied her again. She had a fresh, girl-next-door loveliness, combined with a wry sense of humor that was revealed on her expressive face. "I find that hard to believe," he said.

She shook her head. "Nope. I'm not on very good terms with anyone I've dated before, and I've pretty much ruled out everyone else I know, either for not being presentable or for being likely to take it too seriously. You could say my social life is in a dead zone right now. Even my female friends are all in relationships and busy doing couple things. I've become a fifth wheel." She drained the rest of her glass and gave a little laugh. "You've heard the stereotype of the single woman who lives alone with her cat? Well, I don't even have a cat, just a few sickly houseplants."

"Have you considered getting a cat?" he asked.

She gave him a glare that was diluted by the smile she couldn't quite hold back. "Now, what good would a cat have done me tonight?" she drawled. "It would just give me someone to go home and vent to, and I've got you for that." She swiveled on her stool to face him directly. "And speaking of which, isn't it your turn?"

"My turn?"

"Yeah, remember how this got started?" Now her smile had turned mischievous. Apparently he'd accomplished his goal of cheering her up.

She crossed her legs, which he noticed were nicely shaped, and propped her elbow on the bar, her chin resting in her hand. "We pour out our troubles to each other, then go our separate ways and never see each other again. You've heard my story. What about yours? I'm waiting."

Ken studied the ice cubes in his glass. Now that it was his turn, he found telling his own story a bit more difficult, mainly because he still wasn't sure what exactly he felt. But he had a feeling this woman wouldn't let him rest until he told her at least part of it. And maybe saying it out loud would help clear his thoughts.

"I was at a wedding tonight," he began.

She nodded. "That would explain the outfit. I figured you hadn't been to the rodeo."

He laughed in spite of himself. "Yeah, well, I wish I'd been at the rodeo, or anyplace else. Unfortunately, I agreed to be the best man since it was my best friend's wedding."

"Oh, wedding bells are breaking up that old gang of yours, and it's got you down, huh?"

"Well, not exactly. You see, I know the bride pretty well, too. She's my ex-girlfriend."

She gave a low whistle. "Your ex-girlfriend is marrying your best friend, and you were willing to be best man? I'm impressed. Are you campaigning for sainthood? Most people would have committed murder over something like that."

He shook his head. "That's not a problem. I was the one who broke up with her last year. It just didn't feel right. It sounds kind of silly, but I had an idea of what the right thing would feel like—you know, music, fireworks, and all that. I just needed time and space to make up my mind. Unfortunately, she didn't, and while I was thinking, she moved on to someone else."

He knew he deserved an "It serves you right," but she didn't say anything, just nodded and winced. "I was fine with it, really," he said. "I was happy for them. Up until I saw her walking down that aisle and found myself wishing it was me she was walking to. And now I feel like the biggest jerk in the world."

She patted his arm. "Don't be so hard on yourself. I've known much bigger jerks. Come to think of it, most of them played football." Now it was his turn to glare at her, and she straightened her smile in response. "Have you figured out what exactly is eating you? Is it that you wish you had her, or you wish you weren't the odd one out?"

"I wish I knew. It's just a real pain that as soon as I do make up my mind about what I want, it's too late."

"I think you win this pity party. You have the worst sad story. I'll be fine when I get away from this place, but I'm not so sure about you. You don't seem to have many options at this point, unless you're into home-wrecking."

They'd finished their stories, but Ken wasn't ready to leave. For the first time this evening, he was actually feeling pretty good and enjoying himself. He indicated her empty glass. "Let's not go home just yet. What do you say we make an evening out of this? We'll order another round, find a cozy corner and finish analyzing our sorry states in life."

She hesitated, looking toward the hotel exit, then back at him. Sighing deeply, she shrugged her shoulders and said, "Well, if we're going to wallow in self-pity, we may as well do it right. What the heck. I don't have anyplace else to go tonight, and I'm enjoying the company."

"Another glass of white zinfandel?"

"Sure."

He ordered the drinks from the bartender and they carried them over to a low velvet sofa set in a corner of the hotel lounge. She sat on the sofa and tucked her feet under her. He sat next to her and crossed one ankle over his knee.

In the corner away from the bar, the lighting was more subdued, creating a close, intimate atmosphere. A recessed light in the ceiling above Jenny Forrest's head cast a halo around her. Ken smiled at the image. She was his angel of mercy tonight. Then he glanced at her again and noticed the way her silk dress gently outlined her figure, and his imagery grew a little less heavenly. He shook his head to clear the image and wondered if he'd had a bit too much to drink.

Before his mind could come up with any more crazy images, he cleared his throat. "So," he began. "What's your life story?"

She laughed. "You're going to be bored."

"It can't be that bad. What about all those ex-boyfriends you mentioned, the ones you're not on speaking terms with now? Maybe I could analyze a pattern, figure out where you've gone wrong."

"Oh, so now you're Mr. Fixit instead of just a listening ear."

"Whatever you need."

She took a sip of wine, stared into her glass for a moment, then took a deep breath. "I think the first was the worst. That was way back in college. I was young, lonely and stupid—not the best shape for starting a relationship. Then this guy came along, and it was the first time anyone ever noticed me. It was wonderful—for a couple of months. It went downhill from there, but I was too desperate to just let it go. When it ended, it was ugly."

He nodded. "Yeah, I've seen that happen before."

"So, you see why I'm not on speaking terms with that ex-boyfriend."

"What happened next? Did someone new come along to make you realize the world hadn't ended?"

She laughed, but her laugh had a bitter edge to it. "Not exactly. I didn't date anyone else all that seriously in school. I didn't want to go through that again, and I had learned to be cautious, to make sure I really liked the guy himself instead of liking the fact that he liked me."

"Some people never learn that lesson. When did the next one come along?"

She bent to smooth her stockings, not looking him in the eye. "Oh, about a year or so after I graduated. I was pretty sure this was the one. The timing was right, he was all the things I wanted in a husband. I guess he just didn't see me the same way."

"You guess?"

She shrugged. "That's the best I could do. He never

got around to telling me. In fact, we never actually broke up officially. He just got busy with other things and drifted away until I got tired of it and moved on."

Ken leaned forward. This was getting interesting. "Moved on to where?"

She sighed. "The next one who came along. That didn't last long at all, just long enough for me to feel like I'd made a statement." Rubbing her face with her hands, she groaned and added, "I guess that makes me a user, because he meant no more to me than that, but hey, I was vulnerable."

He had a hard time picturing her as being all that vulnerable. Her emotional armor was so formidable that it was practically visible to the naked eye.

"Then with the last one, it was a complete 180-degree turn from the one before," she went on without prodding. "He was all ready to marry me. I wasn't sure. He couldn't handle that and gave me an ultimatum."

"And you told him to have a good life."

She grinned. "Exactly. So, did you see a pattern there?"

He rubbed his chin, then said in a fake German accent, "I sink you haf bad luck vit men."

She rolled her eyes. "Thanks, Dr. Freud. That's a big surprise to me."

"But seriously, folks," he continued, "I think you figured out the problem with the first one. As for the others, it happens. There are times when you don't like the other person as much as they like you, and vice versa. There's not a lot you can do to control that."

"Okay, so what about you?" she asked.

"Me?"

"Come on, I've told you my life story. How did you get to the point where you are tonight?"

He shook his head. "I already told you. I let her go so I could think. It just didn't feel right—no bells, no violins, none of the things I'd thought of as going along with love. So I decided to look for those things before I made a mistake. While I was looking, so was she, and she seemed to have found them, with my best friend, I might add. And here I am."

"Did you ever find the bells and violins?"

Ken shook his head. "I don't believe they exist anymore." But he could have sworn he was hearing a saxophone, even as he spoke.

2

Jenny couldn't believe she was doing this, sitting in a hotel bar and sharing all the deep secrets of her life with a handsome stranger. What was she thinking? This wasn't like her at all.

She realized now that they'd never even introduced themselves, but it was a little late for that sort of thing, considering the things they'd discussed in the past hour or so. As he had said, it was like talking to a seatmate on an airplane, someone who was quite intimate for a few hours, but once the journey was over would never be seen again.

Already, she felt better for having talked to him, although she wished she'd found him before she'd gone into the reunion. He was quite a catch, tall and dark-haired, with dark gray eyes that made him look mysterious. And the tuxedo didn't hurt either. She wondered if she could slip back into the reunion with him in tow, but she had already been seen alone.

He finished describing his history with the woman he'd let get away. "I know, I sound like a major jerk," he chuckled. "And I'll be the first to say it. I've known this woman almost my entire life, and I still needed time to think about it."

She leaned closer to him and rested her elbow on the

back of the sofa. "You probably don't want to hear this, but if you had to stop and think about it, it may have meant the answer for you was no. If it were right, maybe you wouldn't have had to think."

He rubbed both hands over his face, then through his hair, leaving it standing on end. "Then why do I feel like my life is ending?"

"Weddings are designed to make you feel inadequate if you haven't accomplished the same thing for yourself. Let's face it, the whole world is a conspiracy to make us feel bad about being single."

The melancholy expression on his face lifted for a moment as he raised a skeptical eyebrow. "And how do you figure that?" he asked.

She leaned forward, gesturing with her hands to make her point. "Well, look at it. Most coupons say Buy One, Get One Free. What are you supposed to do if you don't need two? And they look at you funny if you go into a restaurant and ask for a table for one. They don't often hold events you just go to on your own. Radio stations give away sets of two tickets for concerts. You wouldn't think a wedding would make a great date, but they send invitations to single people that say 'and Guest,' so you end up having to find a guest to bring. And you have to be really sure about the emergency stand-by you bring to a wedding. If they don't understand that they're just a warm body to keep you from being an outcast, you could be in trouble. There's something about a wedding that makes single people look at each other differently. If you're not careful, you could end up with a new admirer inspired by the wedding. You could go alone, but because everyone else is there with a date, you're sort of left out in the cold, with nothing to do but eat cake."

He laughed. "Okay, you've got me convinced. They're out to get us. It's a conspiracy."

She smiled, having achieved her goal of getting his mood to lighten a bit. Leaning even closer to him, she lowered her voice to a conspiratorial tone. "But we can fight back, you know. I go to movies alone. I even buy single tickets for the symphony."

"No emergency stand-by needed there, huh?"

"Once they turn the lights down, you might as well be alone. I actually prefer going to movies alone. I can cry without having someone make fun of me, and I don't have to worry about embarrassing moments in the movie, or if the person I'm with is liking it as much as I am."

"There is something to be said for being part of a couple, though," he said, his voice as low as hers. "There are some things you can't do alone."

She knew one major thing that couldn't be done well alone, but she was curious what he meant. "Like what?" she asked.

He winked at her, leaned toward her and whispered, "Oh, lots of things. Like dancing, for example."

She let out a soft sigh of relief. That hadn't been what she expected. "I dance alone all the time. I turn up the radio, dance around my bedroom and serenade my mirror. And even at nightclubs, there are line dances. People seldom really dance together anymore."

He leaned even closer, and when he spoke, his voice was little more than a husky whisper directed straight into her ear. "But it's really hard to slow dance alone. It's just not the same without being cheek to cheek, in each other's arms, feeling each other's heartbeats."

His eyes might still be teasing, but his words and voice made goose bumps rise on Jenny's arms and a shiver go down her spine. "What if I'm not interested in slow dancing? What if I think slow dancing is highly overrated and I'd much rather dance alone?" she whispered, wondering at the odd quiver in her voice.

"Then you've never done it right." He rose from the sofa and extended a hand to help her up. "They're playing our song," he said with a twitch of his head in the direction of the small jazz combo playing in the back corner of the lounge, near the postage-stamp-sized dance floor.

Jenny let him pull her up, although she wasn't sure she liked the idea of dancing when there were no other couples on the floor. The band played a sultry, saxophone-laden version of "The Nearness of You" as he led her to the floor. He put one hand on her back and drew her close while he guided her with his other hand. She put a tentative hand on his shoulder and forced herself to relax into his embrace.

He was tall enough that the top of her head barely came to his chin. She turned her head and rested her cheek against his shoulder. The wool of his tuxedo jacket made her cheek itch, and she could feel the steady thrum of his heart. It wasn't racing, like hers suddenly was. Part of her wanted to tell him that he'd made his point, but then she'd have to move away from him. For now, she felt like she was moving in a dream. It would be over when she woke in the morning, she knew, but for now, she intended to enjoy it. She closed her eyes and allowed him to guide her around the floor. The song came to an end, and he stopped dancing, but continued to hold her close. "See?" he asked.

She nodded and fought to catch her breath. "Okay, you win. Dancing is definitely better done as part of a pair. Now I know what I'm missing."

An older gentleman passed the dance floor, winked at them and gave them a thumbs up. Jenny felt her face grow warm once more. She took a step backward, away from her partner, so they were at least at arm's length.

"Maybe you ought to add danger to your list of requirements for an emergency stand-by," he said, apparently choosing to ignore the fact that she'd moved away from him.

"I think so," she said, forcing her breathing to return to normal. "But that will just make it harder to find a good one."

"I guess it might," he said after a short pause.

She decided against adding that it would also make it more difficult to keep things safe from emotional entanglement. She wouldn't want to give him the wrong impression about what she was feeling at the moment. Taking another step back from him, she said, "There's more to being part of a couple than slow dancing, though. If that's all I have to gain, I may as well stay by myself. Don't tell me dancing is the main thing you miss about your girlfriend."

His brow creased and his eyes narrowed as he took her elbow to lead her back to their seats. For a moment, she wondered if she'd said the wrong thing and made him angry, but after they sat down, he looked at her and said, "No, it's not the dancing. It's just having someone there to share all the little moments of life with. That's what I miss." Sadness and regret reverberated in his voice. In just a short moment, he had gone from being a smooth dance-floor seducer to a hurt little boy who looked as if he'd lost his last friend.

She nodded and patted him on the arm. "I agree. I think the closest I come to feeling like I need someone is when there's something really great that I'd like to share with another person. Otherwise, I'm not likely to get myself involved with someone just so I'll have a date for weddings and office parties.''

He gave her a knowing grin and leaned closer to her. "You just haven't found the right person yet."

She paused a moment before replying, considering her answer. "No, I probably haven't," she said at last. "And I don't intend to tie myself to the wrong person just because I'm alone for the moment."

He tilted his head to one side and let his dark gray eyes scan her up and down. Her skin tingled under his scrutiny. "Is that really the case, or are you being defensive?" he asked after he'd completed his survey.

"What do you mean by that?" she replied, trying to keep her tone even so she wouldn't prove him right by being defensive.

"You're protecting yourself. It's easier to say you don't want to be involved with someone than to feel hurt because you're alone. And it's easier to avoid involvement altogether than to put yourself in a position of getting hurt by loving and losing again."

Now she really had to fight back her instinctive reaction. If she protested too much, he'd think he was close to the truth. She didn't see the point in getting involved with someone who obviously wasn't what she wanted, and she didn't see that as making her overprotective of her feelings, just practical. But she really shouldn't care what he thought, she reminded herself. He wasn't someone she was likely to encounter again. She didn't even know his name.

"What about you?" she riposted. "Aren't you just afraid of commitment? You let your girlfriend get away rather than committing to her, then as soon as she became unavailable, she became much more attractive to you, maybe because there was no longer the risk of a commitment. It's easier to pine over someone you can't have than to get involved with someone who may want some kind of commitment. You can convince yourself that you're ready for involvement, but you're still able to avoid it."

She held her breath, waiting for his reply as his eyes darkened and the creases in his forehead deepened. Suddenly he smiled. "Touché," he said with a bow of his head. "Listen to all this psychobabble we're spouting. I said this would be like therapy, didn't I?"

"And you were right about it being cheaper. But you get what you pay for. I think we're both spending too much time reading self-help books."

"Speak for yourself," he said. "I never read that stuff."

"To be honest, neither do I."

"Good. Then how about another dance?"

Jenny froze at his request. Her physical reaction to the last dance had been almost too much for her to handle with any degree of composure, and she worried that it might be worse the next time. A glance at his face eased her fears somewhat. He was smiling, no sign of intensity or passion. A glance at the main lobby made her decision for her. A group of her former classmates walked past, laughing and talking together. It wouldn't hurt them to see her with someone, as though she had better things to do than mingle at their little reunion.

"One more for the road?" she said with a grin of her own as she took his hand and let him lead her back to the dance floor. Lucky for her, the band was playing a faster song, one that didn't lend itself to steamy slow dancing.

This time, he didn't hold her too closely. Instead, he

was playful, spinning, dipping and twirling her around the floor. She was breathless from exertion and laughter by the time the song ended. He pulled her up from the deep dip he had thrown her into at the end of the song and steadied her while she caught her breath and her balance.

"Whew!" she said when she could talk again. "What happened to all that stuff about slow dancing?"

"You can't be dipped dancing alone, either. I just thought I'd make another point."

"I'm not sure that really adds to your argument. I can live without being dipped all that often. Although I'm sure my chiropractor would love it. He's got a kid going to college."

"But you have to admit that when it's done right, it's classic."

She raised an eyebrow at him. "And I take it that was done right?"

"Your back's not broken, is it? I think we also managed to impress your friends back there."

He had noticed that? She fought back a shudder. Good thing she wasn't likely to run into him again. He was a little too perceptive for her liking. "I don't think they ever thought they'd see me like that," she admitted. "That is, if they even bothered to notice."

"Oh, I'm sure they noticed you. How could they help it with you in that dress?"

This time, he wasn't smiling. He was looking at her with a straight face and an intense gaze. She felt her cheeks grow warm, but she couldn't think of anything to say.

The silence grew heavy as, for the first time in a couple of hours, neither of them had anything to add to the conversation. Jenny decided it was time to end the evening before anything happened to ruin the perfect experience. They'd said everything there was to say, and now it was time to part and return to the real world. If they kept going much longer, one of them was bound to say or do the wrong thing. "I'm really glad I ran into you," she said. "But now I have to go home and water my plants. They get testy when I stay out late and ignore them."

"I can see where that would be something to avoid. Good thing you don't have a cat. That would be even worse. They have claws." He looked awkwardly around the room, then back at her. "It was nice meeting you... uh, I don't think you told me your name."

"We never got around to that, did we? I guess it's a little late for introductions," she laughed nervously. "My name's Jenny."

He shook her hand. "Ken. Well, if you're going to insist on leaving, let me walk you to your car."

"That's not necessary. I valet parked."

"I'll walk you to the valet. Let me do at least that much." He held an arm out for her, and she took it. They walked in silence to the front entrance of the hotel, then he waited with her while the attendant brought her car around.

When she saw her car rounding the corner, she looked up at Ken. "Thank you for listening. I needed a friend tonight, and I had a great time. Thanks to you, the evening wasn't a total disaster and I don't have to go home and cry to my plants."

"And thank you for listening. I'm still a jerk, but at least I feel better about it." He bent to brush his lips lightly against hers. "Have a good life, Jenny."

"You too," she whispered, ducking her head as she went around to the driver's side and got into her car.

She gave him a little wave as she drove off. She could see him in the rearview mirror, still standing beneath the hotel's entrance canopy, his hands shoved deep into the pockets of his tuxedo trousers, until she turned onto the street and headed toward home.

When the hotel was no longer in sight, she sighed and leaned back in her seat, a silly grin on her lips, which still tingled from his light kiss. "Well, now, that was interesting," she said to herself. "Prince Charming still makes the occasional appearance, even if he does turn back into a pumpkin at midnight."

She turned on the radio and scanned the dial for a good, sappy love song to sing along with. Her friends would probably never forgive her for not getting his number, but things were perfect the way they were. If she saw him again under ordinary circumstances, she'd probably find him whiny and annoying. And he probably had terrible fashion sense, so he would never look as suave as he had in that tuxedo. He'd be just like all the other men she'd given up on. He was right about having been a jerk, too. Any man who let the love of his life slip away while he thought it over couldn't be much of a prize outside the confines of a hotel cocktail lounge.

But boy, could he slow dance. Unfortunately, dancing alone would never be quite the same again.

Ken watched the little white Japanese car until its taillights disappeared down the street. "Wow," he said to himself, ignoring the stares of the valet attendants. He didn't know what had possessed him to do any of the things he'd done that night. He hadn't told anyone what he'd discovered about his feelings for Kristen, yet here he had spilled it all to a woman he'd just barely met.

But she'd been easy to talk to, and she was safe. Unlike all his other friends, she didn't know Kristen's side of the story, so he could dwell on his self-pity without recrimination or worry that the story would be passed on to anyone else he knew. And, he wouldn't have to face Jenny again.

He shoved his hands deeper into the pockets of his trousers and strolled back into the lounge. Unfortunately, he'd shared a ride from the church with one of the other groomsmen, and he had to wait until the reception ended before he could leave. He doubted he'd find another pretty, witty woman to help him pass the rest of the evening.

Returning to the bar stool where he'd been sitting earlier, he ordered a club soda with lime. He'd had plenty to drink, and he no longer felt the need to numb any feelings. In fact, he was feeling pretty good, for the time being. He had probably overdone the slow dance, but he'd wanted to show Jenny just how good it could feel. Then, once he realized how good she felt, he had been reluctant to let go. Her body had fit against his perfectly, and the silky fabric of her dress had felt so soft against his hand. It had taken all his will power to keep from stroking it as he held her in his arms. If she had thrown herself at him tonight, he would have been perfectly willing to catch her.

And he couldn't get the sound of distant music out of his head when he thought of her.

He smiled at the memory, only to be startled from his reminiscence by the arrival of his drink. He sipped at it, letting the bubbles of the soda tickle his tongue. As he drank, he caught sight of something in the nearby ashtray. It was a name tag, the one that Jenny had discarded when she entered the lounge.

He returned his attention to his drink and hadn't quite

finished when his friend Rick approached. "You ready to go?"

"Is it over already? Have they left yet?"

"They're staying the night here, so you aren't going to get to throw rice at them. You might as well leave now, unless you want to try for the garter. They'll be tossing it in a few minutes."

"I'll pass. You know what they say about being on the rebound. And the way I feel right now, I feel sorry for the rest of you if I do catch it. You'll never get married." Ken paid his tab, slid off the bar stool and followed Rick to the exit. When they reached the door, he stopped Rick with a hand on his arm and said, "Can you wait a second? I forgot something."

He jogged back to the lounge, where, to his relief, the name tag still sat on the bar where he'd left it. He grabbed it, shoved it into his pocket and returned to the exit. He had no idea why he'd done that, but he hadn't been able to control the impulse. Now he couldn't think of what he'd do with it other than keep it as a memento. They'd already agreed they'd never see each other again. But just in case, he now had a way to try to find her.

3

The phone rang, jolting Ken from his concentration on the notes from his current case. He fumbled for the phone and answered it without lifting his eyes from his legal pad. "Hello?" he said.

"Hello, honey," said the voice on the other end of the line. "Remember me? It's your mother."

Ken groaned and set aside his legal pad. This could take a while, if his mother held true to her usual form. "I'm sorry, Mom, I was going to give y'all a call this weekend."

"I know. You're busy. That's why I called you. If it were up to you, you'd never get around to it."

He knew his mother didn't mean to make him feel bad, even if he did deserve it. "So, what's up? Is everything okay?"

"I was wondering the same about you. Are you going to be joining us for Memorial Day?"

Memorial Day? His parents had hosted a Memorial Day party at their lake property every year for as long as he could remember. He hadn't forgotten the party, but he had forgotten that the coming weekend was Memorial Day. The past couple of weeks had flown as he tried to keep himself busy enough not to think. "Of course I'll be there. I wouldn't miss it."

There was a long pause on the other end of the line. "I ran into Kristen and Greg last weekend. They're back from their honeymoon."

Ken knew that as far as his mother or anyone else knew, he harbored no ill feelings, no regrets. She was merely passing along information. "Oh, how are they?" he asked, keeping his voice as even as he could to avoid betraying the depth of his feelings.

"They looked fine, nice and tan. They must have enjoyed that cruise. They'll be there this weekend."

"Really? I'm looking forward to seeing them again." Ken hoped he wouldn't be struck by lightning for that lie. He wasn't sure how he would react to seeing Kristen as Greg's wife.

"Are you going to be bringing anyone?"

Ken hadn't planned on it, but the last thing he wanted was to be the object of pity at the picnic. All the family friends knew he had dated Kristen for years. They'd be looking to see if he was alone and watching him for signs of regret. "Yeah, I've got a friend I'm planning to bring," he said, upping his lying total for this phone call by one more. His nose was bound to start growing any minute now.

He could almost sense the increased interest coming over the line from his mother. "Oh, really? I can't wait to meet her. And you haven't told me anything about her. I'm shocked."

Well, first he'd have to find her, he thought. At the moment, he didn't know anything to tell since he didn't know who he'd be bringing. "She's just a friend," he hedged, to avoid further interrogation. "And I haven't asked her yet. She may not be able to make it."

"I'm sure she's lovely. I'm looking forward to seeing you."

"Same here, Mom. Sorry I've been out of touch lately."

"I know you're busy, and I'm proud of you. See you this weekend."

Ken hung up the phone with a groan. It was Wednesday. He had four days to find somebody to take to the picnic. What he needed now was one of those emergency stand-by dates that the woman he'd met in the hotel had talked about, someone safe he could call at a time like this.

He sat straight up with a sudden grin. There might be someone for him to invite, after all, if he could find her, and he was sure she was available, unless she'd formed an attachment in the last couple of weeks. He got out of his chair and all but sprinted down the hall to his bedroom. Now, where had he put things when he'd emptied his pockets before returning the rented tuxedo? He searched the top of his dresser, then dug through a couple of drawers before finding the crumpled name tag. He unfolded it, smoothed it out and read it once more: Remember Me? Jenny Forrest, Jacksboro High School. It was the next best thing to a glass slipper.

Forrest was a common enough last name, and Fort Worth was a fairly large city, so he doubted this would be as easy as calling information to get her number. But Jacksboro was a small town, and with any luck, her parents might still live there. With even more luck, they wouldn't immediately suspect him of being a psychopath out to get their lovely daughter.

Assuming he got that far, he wondered how Jenny would react to him calling her. He had been the one to say they could share stories because they'd never see each other again. He wouldn't blame her for being angry. She probably wouldn't have told him half the things she had if she'd thought she'd see him again. He knew he wouldn't have said some things if he'd thought of continuing the relationship.

But she had been smart and funny, which was just what he needed for this event. And she had been the one to define an emergency stand-by date. He knew she'd be able to carry out the role without taking it too seriously.

And maybe if he saw her again in a more normal setting, he could get her out of his mind.

The phone was ringing as Jenny unlocked the front door and staggered into the hallway, her arms laden with grocery bags. One of the bags slipped to the floor at her feet, but it probably contained canned food, so it wouldn't spoil if she left it there. She had enough to carry, as it was, and the phone was still ringing. Hurrying through the hallway to the kitchen, she managed to heave the groceries onto the counter and pick up the phone just before the answering machine came on.

"Hello?" she answered, trying to keep the irritation out of her voice. If this was a telemarketer, she would probably explode.

"Jenny?" said a vaguely familiar male voice on the other end of the line.

Who could this be? She didn't know any men who would be calling her. It had been a long time since that had happened. "Yes, this is Jenny," she said. "Can I help you?"

"Well, uh, this is Ken, from the hotel. Your class reunion, my ex-girlfriend's wedding. Remember me?"

Jenny had to grab the kitchen counter to steady herself as her legs suddenly went watery and her stomach lurched. She hadn't expected to hear from him again. In fact, she hadn't thought she'd given him enough information to find her. If she'd thought he'd be calling her a couple of weeks later, she wouldn't have told him half the things she had.

"Yeah, I remember you," she said cautiously as she took the phone over to a chair where she could sit down and get off her suddenly unsteady legs. What could he want from her?

"I hope I didn't startle you."

"Oh, just a little bit. Do you happen to work for the CIA?"

He laughed, and his laugh sounded almost as nervous as she was feeling. "In other words, how did I find you? You left your name tag on the bar and I took it with me, for some odd reason. Then when I decided I wanted to find you again, I found your parents in Jacksboro and once they'd determined that I wasn't going to stalk you and that I seemed like a nice, honest young man, they gave me your number. Mind you, that did take nearly an hour, and I had to promise never to keep you out late."

Jenny felt a little bit better knowing that he'd had to go through her parents to find her, but her head was still swimming. He wasn't supposed to show up in her life again, especially not through any effort on his part. If they'd just happened to meet again, it would be fate, but this risked damaging an evening that had been perfect for her. She hated it when reality got in the way of a good fantasy.

"Wow," she said in response to his story. "You must have really needed to talk to me. Did another old girlfriend get married?"

He laughed again. "No, no more ex-girlfriends to send me plunging into depression. I hope this doesn't make you think I'm lonely and pathetic, but what I need right now is one of your emergency stand-by dates."

"Emergency stand-by dates?" she heard herself parroting. So far, she was hardly the brilliant conversationalist she had managed to be that night at the hotel.

"Yeah. Every year, my folks hold a big picnic and party at the lake for Memorial Day. And guess who's always invited."

"And guess who's going to have her new husband there this year," she finished for him. "And guess who doesn't want to have to face the happy couple as the lonely single guy too pitiful to get a date for the picnic."

"Are you some kind of mind reader? You have that down perfectly."

"Let's just say I've been there more than once."

"So, would you be interested in being an emergency stand-by date for me? You're the only one I can think of. I can return the favor sometime if you need it."

She wasn't sure whether to be flattered or insulted that she was his desperation measure. "Memorial Day, you said?" she hesitated, as if she really had plans that didn't involve lying around the house watching old movies on television or going to visit her parents. "I guess I could make it. About what time?"

"We usually get started around five. It's really casual. Shorts, T-shirts, that sort of thing. Bring a swimsuit if you want to go swimming or waterskiing." He sounded so hopeful she could hardly turn him down. And he had saved her sanity that evening. If she hadn't run into him, she would have gone home, pigged out on ice cream and cried herself to sleep, just as she had so many times in high school. Instead, she had gone home feeling sexy and confident.

"Yes, I suppose I can make it," she said, keeping a

hint of distance in her voice. She didn't want him to think she was eager to see him again.

"Great! Where can I pick you up?"

"Why don't we meet somewhere neutral? You may have impressed my parents, but I'd feel more comfortable not giving away the location of my secret lair just yet."

"I can understand that. What about the parking lot at the Eagle Mountain Lake marina?" he suggested. "About five on Monday."

"Sounds good. Do I need to bring anything?"

"Just yourself. My mother has had this planned for months. She's a born hostess."

"Well, I guess I'll see you then," she said.

"Thanks so much, Jenny. I really do owe you one," he said before hanging up.

Jenny put down the phone and started putting away her groceries. She was shaking, but whether it was because she'd insisted on carrying all her groceries at once from the store to the car, and then from the car into the house, or because of the sudden reappearance of Ken in her life, she wasn't sure. It was difficult to sort out her feelings. She had liked Ken, and it was a pleasant surprise that he had been interested enough to go to all the effort of tracking her down. But he had called her to be an emergency stand-by date, and according to the definition she had given him, that meant a safe date who knew better than to expect anything lasting in a relationship. So, right from the start, she knew she wasn't a contender. Besides, if he'd been truly fascinated, he would have tracked her down sooner, or even asked for her number that night at the hotel.

But that shouldn't bother her. That was all she wanted right now, just someone to go with her to events where an escort was mandatory. This should be just what she needed. It was the ideal relationship for this phase in her life.

At any rate, she needed something new to wear. After all, she'd be meeting his parents, and she knew he'd want to show her off to the old girlfriend. She grinned, thinking that she could play that game well enough. Ken should enjoy this.

On Memorial Day afternoon, Jenny smoothed the front of her new light blue shorts and leaned against the hood of her car, trying to look much more cool and casual than she felt. She had deliberately arrived early so she could prepare herself mentally for Ken's arrival. Butterflies performed acrobatic maneuvers in her stomach. She had never done anything like this before. Several times during the past few days, she would have been tempted to cancel the date if she'd had any way to contact Ken.

But she hadn't, so she was trying to make the best of it. She had agonized long and hard over what to wear, knowing that definitions of casual varied widely, but had settled on a crisp pair of shorts that were long enough for decorum but short enough to show off her legs, a sleeveless white cotton blouse and ballerina flats. She had styled her hair in a French braid, and a dose of self-tanning lotion gave her skin a light bronze glow she never managed to get from the sun itself.

She was ready for this, although she had to remind herself that she shouldn't be nervous about meeting the parents of someone she wasn't dating seriously. As each car pulled into the parking lot, her heartbeat sped up slightly until the car passed her by. Finally, a sleek black sports car drove up and slowed down as it approached her. Then it pulled into a parking space next to her, and Ken emerged.

He was as good-looking as she remembered, tall, dark-haired, with a lean build, although in shorts and a polo shirt, he looked quite a bit different than he had in a tux. He looked more normal, less as if he belonged in a scene from *Casablanca*. Instead of disappointment at seeing him in something closer to the real world, she felt relief at seeing that he hadn't transformed into something terribly mundane. He was someone she might have noticed no matter where she met him.

He gave her a nervous smile that told her he felt as awkward about this as she did. Strangely enough, that made her feel better.

"Hi, Jenny," he said, moving toward her, then stopping at arm's reach. "It's great to see you again."

"Yeah," she replied, not sure yet whether it was really great or not. She had a hard time looking into his eyes, knowing he knew far more about her than even her closest friends.

His smile faded and he glanced away, not meeting her eyes, either. "Hey, I really appreciate you doing this. I meant what I said about returning the favor. Let me know if you need anything."

She shrugged, trying to look more casual than she felt. She wondered if her legs looked as quivery as they felt. "No problem. It gives me something to do." She flashed him a quick grin. "And my mother is delighted that a man went to so much effort to ask me out. She's feeling a lot better about her chances of someday becoming a grandmother. I'm letting her enjoy her little fantasy. Unfortunately, she's now dying to meet you."

He laughed. "Your mother sounds a lot like mine. I guess that's one of the reasons I wanted to bring someone tonight. Otherwise, I'd hear no end of comments about how I really need to find a nice girl because I'm not getting any younger."

"So, your mother owes me one, too," Jenny replied with a grin.

"Don't worry, her blackberry cobbler will more than settle the debt." He moved around to the other side of the car and opened the door for her. "I guess we should get going."

She moved forward and lowered herself into the car's leather bucket seat, then buckled her seat belt while he ran back around the car and took his own seat. "It's not too far from here," he assured her as he started the car and drove away from the marina.

As the car sped down the winding lakeside road, Jenny cast a sidelong glance at Ken. "This is kind of an awkward question," she said after a few moments of silence, "but what kind of intimacy are we to assume?"

"What?" He whirled to look at her so sharply she was afraid he would run the car off the road.

"Well, somehow I doubt you want to be perfectly open about the fact that we've met only once before and I'm just your emergency stand-by date because you don't want to face your ex-girlfriend alone."

He gave her a shaky smile. "I honestly hadn't thought about that. I told my mother you were just a friend. She'll probably interpret that to mean that you're a bit more than a friend, but I'm being cautious because this is too important to move quickly. So, that might be a good approach. We haven't been dating long and are more friends than anything else."

"I take it that means no really mushy stuff, no long, lingering glances and no major displays of public affection. Just a few quick glances and minor touches. We like each other, but it hasn't gone further yet."

He laughed. "That should work. You even wrote the script."

"Okay, then, I'm ready."

A few minutes later, when they reached Ken's parents' lake property, she wasn't so sure how ready she was. Their lake house was bigger than her own parents' regular house. Just who was this guy, anyway?

A slender woman with salt-and-pepper hair met them before they made it beyond the driveway. She greeted Ken with a hug and a kiss, then turned to survey Jenny with an analytical gaze. Apparently she passed muster, for the woman then gave Jenny a warm smile and took her hand in both of hers. "It's so nice to meet you..." she let the sentence trail off, looking expectantly back at Ken.

"Jenny Forrest, as I would have managed to introduce her if you'd waited five seconds before giving the poor woman the third degree. Jenny, this is my mother, Ellen. Don't let her bother you."

"I'm not bothering her. You make me sound like a scary dog that jumps on guests. I'm just being nice to your friend."

"No comment," Ken said, raising one eyebrow and winking at Jenny, who couldn't help but laugh at the interplay between mother and son. Underneath the banter, she detected a loving relationship.

Ellen put one arm around Jenny's shoulders and walked with her to the house. "If he keeps this up, you and I may have to find my secret stash of baby pictures," she said.

"Hey!" he shouted in protest, hurrying to catch up with them. "That's not fair."

Jenny had to grin, but she really hoped it was just a joke. She wasn't quite sure she was ready for naked pictures of Ken—no matter how young he was in the photos. She knew far too much about him already.

They went around to the back of the lake house to where a redwood deck stretched from the edge of the backyard out over the lakeshore. A couple of motorboats were tied up to the deck. A picnic canopy had been staked out in the yard, with tables laden with food underneath. Nearby, a man in a rakishly tilted chef's hat and an apron reading "The danger makes it taste better" tended hamburgers and hot dogs on a grill.

Jenny heard Ken groan behind her. "I can't believe he's wearing that," he said.

Ellen chuckled. "You gave it to him. What do you expect?"

"There should be some kind of statute of limitations on childhood presents," Ken insisted.

The man at the grill waved a spatula at them. "So, Ken, this is your mystery woman," he shouted.

Ken winced. "Dad, this is Jenny Forrest. Jenny, this is my father, John. Please excuse the apron. I gave it to him when I was ten, and he won't grill without it."

Jenny grinned. "Nice to meet you," she said, fighting to stifle a laugh. Ken's parents might have impressive resources, but they had a goofy sense of humor that immediately brought them down to earth for her. She relaxed tremendously. This might not be so bad, after all.

"Ken, why don't you take Jenny and get her something to drink. It's hot out here. There's some lemonade and iced tea under the picnic tent," Ellen said with a pat on Jenny's shoulder. "The rest of the guests should be here soon."

"That means she and Dad want to compare notes about you," Ken translated. He guided Jenny toward the canopy with a hand at her elbow. "Sorry about that," he said softly when they were out of earshot of his parents. "I should have warned you about them."

"They're not so bad. At least they're not stiff and frightening."

"Just wait. They haven't started on you yet. But don't worry, you don't have to answer any questions without your attorney present."

"I take it that means I can expect to be interrogated during the evening."

"The FBI has nothing on those two. They're going to try to separate us and quiz you about me and the prospects for our relationship. That's why I said not to answer questions without your attorney present."

"And who would that attorney be?"

"Me."

An attorney, Jenny thought. Normally considered a big prize, but she wasn't sure she liked the reputation of the profession. If he was a nice guy, he couldn't be a very good attorney, and if he was a good attorney, it wasn't likely he was a very nice guy.

She must have showed her displeasure in her face, for he clapped her on the back and said, "We don't all drip slime behind us when we walk. I like to think of myself as one of the good guys."

"I don't know. That's the kind of thing that should be disclosed up front, don't you think? It could have been a factor in my decision." She raised an eyebrow at him, but couldn't keep a smile from twisting her lips.

"Did you tell that to my parents when you were trying to get my number?"

"I'm not that foolish," he said with a grin. They reached the picnic canopy, and he handed her a glass of lemonade. "I don't know what you do, either," he said, looking her straight in the eye.

"There's a lot you don't know about me." *And far too much that you do know about me,* she thought.

"Don't get coy. What about it? They'll probably ask me, anyway," he said with a glance in the direction of his parents, "and it would look bad if I didn't know."

"I work in advertising," she admitted.

"That's almost as bad as law," he said with a teasing smile.

"I don't think so. We just convince people that they need things they don't. You benefit from other people's misfortune. Besides, I don't do the actual advertising. I work on the management end of things. I just convince companies to spend money on advertising. I don't create the actual misleading ads."

He raised his hands in mock submission. "I'll take your word for it. You're less of a detriment to mankind than I am."

A shout from across the yard interrupted their conversation. Jenny watched Ken's eyes stray from her face to a spot in the distance. She turned her head to see Ellen running to embrace a tall, blond young woman and an equally tall, blond young man.

Jenny glanced back at Ken to see the muscles in his jaw tighten. Without him saying a word, she knew who the new arrivals were. So, this was the woman who had ruined Ken's life. "Okay, I guess it's show time," she said.

He shot her a look that was somewhere between a

glare and a hint of stark terror, then put his arm around her shoulders and began moving the two of them over to greet the newcomers. Jenny had to hurry to keep up with him. It seemed to her he was more interested in reaching Kristen than in staying with her. Then again, what did she expect? She was here just to be shown off to Kristen.

By the time they reached Kristen and her husband, Ken had schooled his features into a mask of pleasure. "Kristen, Greg, it's great to see you. I'd like you to meet Jenny." He gave Jenny a big squeeze around the shoulders, drawing her up against his side so sharply that it almost made her gasp.

Noting how quickly Kristen's eyes cut to study her, Jenny put on her biggest "I'm in love" smile and gazed adoringly up at Ken. It didn't require too much acting ability to admire him. And it wouldn't be too hard to allow herself to enjoy this game, even if it lasted for just one night. She'd have to keep reminding herself that this was all there would be. It wouldn't do to get lost in her role.

4

Ken held on to Jenny like a lifeline until he got past the initial shock of seeing Kristen again. He forced himself to smile, only to realize his face was already frozen into a smiling mask. "How are you?" he asked.

Kristen squeezed her husband's arm and smiled. "We're great. And you?"

"I'm fine. Just fine." He squeezed Jenny's shoulders and gazed down at her, as if in adoration. He couldn't help but notice the "we" as one more reminder that she was now linked to Greg.

Kristen raised an eyebrow, and he panicked at the thought that she might have seen through his act. He relaxed when she said, "Was I just so caught up in the wedding that I didn't notice her there with you, or have I not met Jenny yet? I can't believe you didn't tell me about her."

He opened his mouth to explain, but no words came out. He couldn't think of a thing to say.

"Ken's so considerate," Jenny said, looking up at him with admiration in her eyes. "He thought it would be too awkward for me to have to go to a wedding of people I didn't know and sit alone in the church while he was up front playing best man. So he told me he didn't expect me to go, and we'd get together later." She giggled and gave him a quick hug. "It's okay, I still got to see him in his tux."

Ken could have kissed her. That was better than anything he could have come up with. On second thought, he should kiss her, he decided, and he bent to kiss her forehead. Then he looked back at Kristen to see her reaction.

She was smiling. Not a jealous smile, just an "I'm happy for you" smile. He looked back down at Jenny and caught what might have been a sly wink. Fighting back a laugh, he felt the tension flow out of him. This wasn't so bad, he thought. It was hardly the end of the world he'd been picturing for weeks.

Then he couldn't help wondering why he'd been so anxious about this moment. It was anticlimactic, to say the least. Kristen seemed genuinely glad to see him, and not the least bit jealous of Jenny. Without the wedding gown, she lost the otherworldly quality she'd had a couple of weeks ago, and now she was just ordinary Kristen again. He had loved her once, he supposed. Actually, he still did love her, but more the way one loved a sister. And he didn't hear any music at all.

He had to fight back an idiotic grin. Now he really felt like a fool. He had plunged himself into depression over this? Jenny had been right. He had just wanted something merely because he could no longer have it. It was just one more case of him making snap judgments with his heart before his brain was able to kick into gear. Good thing it was a habit he had given up.

Now much more at ease, he motioned toward the grill. "I think Dad is almost through burning the burgers," he said. "What do you say we get something to eat, and then we can all sit and get caught up. I'd like to hear all about your honeymoon—well, not all," he hurried to add when both Kristen and Jenny's cheeks flushed bright red.

Real smooth, he scolded himself. Now that he had his life back in perspective, he shouldn't be acting like an idiot. By this time, Jenny probably thought he was in serious need of professional psychological help. And maybe she was right.

Kristen, who by this time knew him well enough to know his mouth and brain sometimes operated independently, jumped in to turn the moment into something approaching a reasonable conversation. "So, Jenny, how long have you known Ken?" she asked.

"Not too long," Jenny replied with a shy smile that created dimples at the corners of her mouth. He'd never noticed she had dimples before. Then he reminded himself he'd only spent a few hours with her before now. It just seemed as if he knew her better.

"How did you meet?" Kristen continued.

Jenny glanced up at Ken, a flash of panic in her eyes. "Oh, it wasn't anything exciting. We just got started talking and…"

"We haven't stopped since then," Ken finished, smiling down at Jenny and giving her a quick kiss on the temple.

Now Jenny was edging away from him, as if she was afraid she'd accepted a date with a nutcase. Fortunately, they had reached the grill and his father was depositing grayish-brown disks on plates for them. It really was a shame his mother let his father cook at these picnics. The burgers were always in sharp contrast to the rest of the meal. But she said a little indigestion was a small price to pay for letting him feel like a great chef for one afternoon out of the year.

They moved on to the table spread with condiments

and fixings. "Don't worry," he whispered to Jenny. "If you put enough ketchup on them, they're not so bad."

"That's not what I'm worried about," she whispered back at him. "Are you okay? You're acting really strange. Not that I know you well enough to know what strange is," she added with a shrug. "This may be normal for you."

"I'm fine, really," he assured her. "In fact, I'm feeling wonderful."

"I think maybe you'd better sit down in the shade," she shot back. "You're most certainly not fine. Are you light-headed?"

As a matter of fact, he was. He felt like a tremendous weight had been lifted from his shoulders. He wanted to sing and dance—although if he did, Jenny would probably run screaming in fear. But how else was he to react to realizing he hadn't ruined his life, after all?

He led Jenny to a picnic table, where Kristen and Greg joined them a moment later. By then, he'd managed to steady his thoughts enough to stop babbling like an idiot. The four of them chatted until one of the other guests paused by the table to greet the newlyweds.

Jenny snatched a potato chip off Ken's plate and studied him carefully as she chewed. "Okay, you seem a bit saner now," she said softly after finishing her perusal. "You must be getting enough oxygen to the brain."

She glanced over her shoulder at Kristen, who was deep in conversation with the newcomers. "So, that's the dream girl you can't have? She seems nice. Hardly worth ruining your life over, but then, what woman is?"

He wasn't sure how to answer that. He settled for shrugging his shoulders and saying, "Okay, so maybe I overreacted just a bit."

"Overreacted? I thought you were going to throw yourself off a bridge."

"I wasn't that bad. I was just a little moody."

She smirked at him, "If you insist. But if that's a little moody, I don't want to be around you when you're really being moody."

Her smirk quickly turned into a bright smile, and Ken turned to notice that Kristen and Greg had returned their attention to them, the other guests having moved on to the food line. He glanced back at Jenny, who looked suitably love-struck. She was far too good at that. Even he might have been convinced if he hadn't seen her smirking at him a few seconds ago.

An awkward silence hung over the table as none of them could think of anything to say. Ken forced a smile and said, "How was the honeymoon? No hurricanes or other disasters?"

"Not even missing luggage," Kristen replied. "It was nice."

"It was more than nice," Greg said, slipping his arm around Kristen's shoulders.

Next to Ken, Jenny coughed. He turned just in time to catch her rolling her eyes. He had to bite his lip to keep from grinning. Greg must really deserve Kristen, Ken decided. He had never managed to be that lovesick over her. But as free as he now felt, he didn't care to spend much more time with the cooing newlyweds. Shoving aside his half-eaten hamburger, he said, "It looks like the Johnsons are here. I'd like you to meet them, Jenny, if you're through eating."

She gave her burger a critical glance, then stood up and took his hand. He led her just out of earshot then let his breath out with a sigh. "Whew! I wasn't sure how much more of that I could take."

She patted him on the shoulder. "That must have been rough. But you handled it fairly well, aside from the babbling at the start. No one would have guessed what you were going through."

He started to ask what she meant, then remembered that as far as she knew, he was still in love with Kristen. He opened his mouth to tell her, but she slipped one arm around his waist and leaned her head against his shoulder. She was playing her part well. With a glance over his shoulder at Kristen and Greg, who were too caught up in each other to notice him, he draped his arm awkwardly around Jenny's shoulder. It settled there nicely. In fact, this felt pretty good. It was just for this evening, he reminded himself, but for now, they might as well enjoy themselves.

Jenny surprised herself with how well she was playing her role. Normally she liked to keep a safe distance from people she didn't know well, but here she was, cuddling against Ken. And enjoying it, she realized. She didn't even mind meeting the parade of relatives and family friends, although she knew she'd never remember their names. Ken introduced her to them all as if he was genuinely proud of having found her.

After meeting what seemed like the final newcomers to the party, Ken led her to the drink table and handed her a cup of lemonade. He took one, then they walked out onto the dock, where he sat down with a deep sigh and patted the plank next to him. She sat down in the spot he indicated on the sun-warmed wood. "I believe the worst is over, so we might as well retreat," he said.

"This wasn't so bad," she said. "I don't see what you were dreading."

"It wasn't so bad because you were here. Everyone

was too busy asking about you to wonder what happened with Kristen. If you hadn't been here, no one might have said anything to me, but behind my back they'd all be saying things like, 'Poor Ken, I don't know how he's handling Kristen being married to Greg. I can't believe the fool boy was stupid enough to let her go.'"

She raised an eyebrow at him. "What do you think they're saying behind your back now?"

"They're wondering if I'm going to be stupid enough to let another wonderful woman get away from me."

She looked over her shoulder back at the lawn and noticed that Ken's parents glanced toward the dock every so often. "You're not going to get a lot of grief from your parents when I'm not around after this, are you?" she asked.

He grinned. "I'll just tell them they scared you away. I'll get plenty of guilt mileage out of that."

Laughing, she leaned against him, conscious of the fact that they were being watched from the shore. He was strong and solid, and it felt good to rest against someone else—even if this was just an act. "It's peaceful out here," she said with a soft sigh. "Just the water, the trees…"

"And about fifty guests." He finished her sentence.

"But I can almost forget they're all there."

"Well, they are. And for some of them, we're the main attraction. What do you say we put on a show?"

She wasn't sure what he had in mind, but her pulse sped up as she nodded. He put his arm around her and ran one finger up and down her arm, slowly. It was enough to send a shiver up her spine. Then he brushed a stray tendril of hair away from her face and bent to kiss her. He wouldn't have to kiss her much to give the right effect for those watching from the shore, and at first it seemed he was only going to brush her lips lightly with his. But then he kissed her again, more firmly. And before she was aware of what she was doing, she was kissing him in return. His lips were warm and soft, and seemed to set hers on fire. When the kiss had gone on long enough that it would really be raising eyebrows back on shore, he broke off the kiss.

They looked into each other's eyes for a long moment, both breathing heavily. Waves slapped against the pilings of the dock, punctuating each second as it passed. Then Ken cracked a grin and said, "There, that should give them plenty to talk about. It'll be enough to keep Mom going for weeks."

"I'm going to hate having to break that poor woman's heart," Jenny said when she trusted herself enough to talk again. She didn't know what that kiss had done to Ken, but it had her feeling wobbly. Then again, it had been far too long since she had been kissed at all. She was probably out of practice. "Your mom is going to be disappointed when she finds out she's not going to be a grandmother soon, after all."

"At least she'll have a few weeks of happiness, which buys me a little more time."

Jenny wanted to ask what he was planning to do with the time he'd gained, but she was afraid she knew what the answer would be. He'd spend the time finding someone he really liked. She didn't know why that thought bothered her so much. She was just playing a part here.

He moved a little farther from her, but stayed near enough to seem close to the audience watching from the backyard. "You never did tell me if you felt better after that night," he said after a few moments of silence.

"I was fine by the time I left the hotel, thanks to you.

I just won't put myself through that again. For the twenty-year reunion, I'll find a date or I won't go at all."

"Maybe you should start looking for emergency stand-by dates to keep handy, just in case."

"What are you doing ten years from now?" she asked with a wink.

"My calendar doesn't go that far into the future. I did say I owed you one after bringing you out here, but I was thinking of repaying the favor a little sooner."

She glanced over her shoulder back at the shore and relaxed when she saw that they were no longer being watched. "I think we're finally offstage," she said.

"We can't have that, now, can we?" he said with a grin, standing and extending a hand to help her up. He kept his grip on her hand as they walked down the dock back to the shore.

"Don't you think we've been convincing enough?" she hissed at him. "You've thoroughly thrown people off the path. They'll never guess at your true feelings."

"You think so?"

She nodded. If he kissed her one more time, she would have a very hard time reminding herself that this was all an act.

"Are you ready to go home?" he asked.

"Probably. If you don't mind?"

"Frankly, I'd welcome an excuse to escape."

"Then I guess we'd better say good-night to your folks."

He escorted her to where his parents stood chatting with neighbors. Jenny stepped forward and said, "Thank you so much for having me tonight. I had a wonderful time."

"Don't tell me you're leaving already!" Ellen exclaimed.

"Mom, Jenny was kind enough to join us. Don't ask her to move in," Ken said with a stern edge in his voice and a glint of a grin in his eyes.

"That sounds like a good idea," Ellen said, winking at Jenny. She hugged Jenny, adding, "It was so nice to meet you, dear. Please come back soon. We'll have to invite you over for lunch sometime, when there won't be so many others and we can talk."

Jenny made a noncommittal noise in her throat that could be taken either way. She was already worried about how Ken was going to explain the fact that she wasn't around anymore. She didn't want to give him more to deal with.

Both she and Ken gave deep sighs of relief as they buckled themselves into Ken's car. "Well, it looks like we made it," she said, turning to him.

"Yeah. We did." He started the car and drove away. Jenny waited for him to say something else, but he didn't. She looked down to notice his hand resting on the gearshift. She had a sudden urge to rest her hand on top of his, but then she reminded herself that the show was now over. They were offstage, and she didn't need to go on acting the dutiful girlfriend.

"Actually, it wasn't so painful," she said, just to keep the silence in the car from overpowering her. "Your family seems nice."

"They're not so bad, I suppose," he said with a brief flash of grin. "But thanks for putting up with it all. I really appreciate it. You saved my life."

"I don't think it was as dire as all that. You're a big boy. You could have handled it."

"But it wouldn't have been as easy. Or as much fun."

"Well, anytime you need me," she started to say, then

corrected herself. "Not around your family again, though. I don't want to give them the wrong idea."

"Remember, though, I owe you. You get the next emergency date."

She wasn't sure when that would be. Knowing her luck, he'd have hooked up with someone else the next time she needed a date.

He pulled into the parking lot where she'd left her car. Before opening the door, he took a pen and a scrap of paper from the glove compartment and wrote something. He handed it to her and said, "I mean it, I owe you. Call me if you need me." She glanced at the paper to see his name and phone number written on it. Folding it carefully, she put it in her pocket.

He got out of the car, then opened her door and helped her out. He walked with her to her car and waited while she opened the door. She turned around to face him. "Thanks for inviting me," she said. "I really did have a good time."

"No, thank you for coming. I'm glad you introduced the stand-by date concept to me." He stepped forward and she held her breath. If he kissed her again, she wasn't sure how she would react. But he didn't. He just grinned at her, thanked her once more, then walked back to his car. Jenny got into her car before her legs buckled under her. She felt wilted from disappointment, although she wasn't sure why. It had all been an act in front of the guests. Why would he need to continue the act here in a dark, abandoned parking lot?

As she turned out of the parking lot, she could see his taillights disappear in the opposite direction.

Holding the steering wheel with one hand, she felt for the slip of paper she'd put in her pocket. Too bad she couldn't think of any impending social obligations, but it was probably for the best. With Ken, she knew up front that he was a broken heart waiting to happen. Already she was feeling wilted because he hadn't kissed her good-night. She could imagine what she'd feel if she were any more involved.

If she had reason to call him, she'd better remind herself of her own stand-by date definition.

As soon as he was away from the marina parking lot, Ken slapped his palm against the steering wheel. "What got into me?" he said out loud. He'd been crazy in so many ways tonight, he didn't know where to begin.

First, there was the whole thing with Kristen. He was still reeling from that revelation. All the time he'd spent mourning the loss of her from his life, and it had been his typical overreaction. If he needed any more reason to change his ways, that had been it.

But he hadn't learned from that experience, apparently. He didn't know what he was thinking when he'd kissed Jenny. That hadn't been on his agenda for the evening. He didn't exactly regret it. It had been nice—more than nice—but it hadn't been smart, as confused as he already was.

It hadn't been fair to Jenny, either. He'd told her all she had to be was a friend, with nothing more expected of her. Then he'd gone and kissed her like that. He was bad news when it came to women, but surely Jenny was bound to know that, too, after all he'd told her. He felt a bit better, realizing that. Jenny was a smart woman. She knew well enough that their kiss didn't mean anything and that she couldn't expect more from him.

Ken also had a feeling he wouldn't be seeing her again. After the way he'd acted tonight, he doubted she'd call him, no matter how desperate she got for a stand-by date.

5

"Not another wedding invitation," Jenny groaned, glaring at the cream-colored envelope with her address written on it in calligraphy. There was nothing else it could be—no one sent formal, engraved invitations to casual get-togethers. In the past year or so, she had grown to dread weddings. It meant a Saturday afternoon wearing uncomfortable clothes and talking to people she didn't know well, while the person who knew her well enough to want her to share this special day was too busy to notice her presence. Meanwhile, the whole event seemed arranged to point out that if you weren't married yet, that should be your goal.

She dropped her briefcase in the front hallway of her house and sorted through the rest of her mail. It was mostly bills and advertising circulars. Then she forced herself to open the cream envelope. Inside was another envelope, addressed to Jennifer and Guest. "...and Guest" were the two words she most hated to see written in calligraphy. Weddings always made for awkward dates. Everyone seemed to take great delight in hinting that every couple there should be planning their own wedding, and the romantic setting was likely to put thoughts into dates' heads, whether or not the relationship had really progressed to that level.

She opened the inner envelope to find out whose wedding it was. Lori Jenson wasn't a close friend—Jenny had served on a church committee with her once—but all her friends from church would be at the wedding—with dates, of course. Which meant that if she went alone again, she'd be stuck either talking to the weird relative everyone else avoided or standing by the buffet table, stuffing her face. No, she wasn't going to face this one alone.

She took the invitation with her into the kitchen to check her schedule on the calendar that hung on the refrigerator door. With any luck, she'd already be busy, so she wouldn't have to worry about it.

Nope, her schedule was clear, Jenny realized with a sigh. Then she looked up to see the slip of paper with Ken's name and number stuck to the refrigerator door with a magnet shaped like a hamburger. She pulled the paper loose from the magnet and studied it. Did she know him well enough to invite him to a wedding? Or did she know him too well? She shivered as she remembered the kiss he'd given her out on the dock.

Then she remembered the kiss he hadn't given her, in the parking lot. It didn't look as if she was in any danger of him taking the wedding too seriously, and she had to admit that he was presentable in public. He was also fun, which should make the wedding a little less unpleasant.

She reached for the phone, then decided to wait until a little later. Maybe she'd call him after dinner. He'd said he was an attorney, so he was probably working late.

She got out of her work clothes and into shorts and a T-shirt, then microwaved a frozen dinner and ate while she read the newspaper. She cleaned up after dinner, straightened the living room, and watched a situation comedy on television. Finally, she decided she couldn't put it off any longer. She had to call him.

Steeling her resolve, she marched into the kitchen, took the number off the refrigerator door, picked up the phone and dialed, before she could change her mind. She held her breath while she listened to the phone ring and waited for someone to answer.

Ken absently nibbled on a take-out burger while he reviewed a deposition transcript and made notes. He was so deep in concentration that he jumped when the phone rang. While he finished chewing his last bite, he fumbled behind him for the phone that hung on the kitchen wall. "Hello?" he answered, his mind still focused on his work.

"Um, Ken?" said a hesitant voice on the line. "This is Jenny. Remember me?"

He sat straight up, shoving aside his work. "I was wondering if you'd forgotten me," he said.

She laughed, a tight, nervous sound, and said, "I know it's been a while, but my social calendar slowed down a little bit, so your services weren't required."

He'd thought about calling her when he hadn't heard from her, then he'd thought better of it. The last thing he needed was yet another headlong plunge into a new relationship before he finished recovering from the last one. "I take it something just landed on your calendar," he said.

"Yeah, and remember, you did say you'd return the favor."

"Gladly. Just tell me when, where and appropriate attire."

"Two weeks from Saturday. Four p.m. It's a wedding, so attire appropriate for the occasion."

A wedding wasn't on top of his list of things he wanted to do on a date, but then again, it could be a good idea, considering his circumstances. Jenny herself had said that a stand-by wedding date had to be the safest date of all because of the danger of the date getting too many romantic thoughts into his head. Well, now he knew what she thought of him. He was safe, which meant he wasn't the only one trying to avoid entanglements right now. Next thing he knew, she'd be saying he was like a brother to her, and for the first time in his life, that sounded good.

"I believe I can make that," he said.

"Oh, good!" She sounded genuinely relieved, and he felt a sting. Had she thought he wouldn't be true to his word? He might have painted himself as a jerk, but he'd like to think he was a chivalrous one.

"Where is this wedding?" he asked.

"It's at a church downtown. It won't be too formal, just the usual coat and tie."

"Do you trust me enough by now to let me pick you up, or do you want to meet somewhere?"

There was a long pause on the other end of the line while she made up her mind. "I live pretty close to the university," she finally said. "Not in the really fancy neighborhood, but farther away, in one of the smaller, old houses." She gave him directions, which he took down on his legal pad.

"That's not too far from where my parents live. I don't think I'll have any trouble finding it. I'll pick you up at around three."

"Thanks, Ken. I really appreciate this. And you won't have to put on a big boyfriend act for me there. No one is expecting anything. I just need someone to talk to so I'm not stuck entertaining Great-Aunt Bertha who has managed to insult everyone in her family and can't find anyone to talk to.''

He laughed. She might not need him to be a boyfriend, but if he did his job, he might be able to improve her social life a bit. "No problem. I'll see you then," he said before hanging up the phone. There was nothing like being seen with an interested man to attract the interest of other men. He grinned as his plan began developing in his mind.

Jenny couldn't believe she'd bought a new dress to go to the wedding of someone who wasn't particularly close to her. She studied her reflection in the cheval glass and frowned. Away from the store, she wasn't sure the floral print dress was right for her. She wasn't normally given to feminine flounces, but this dress had a garden-party style that had appealed to her when she first saw it. Now she thought maybe it was overkill. Just as she started to consider changing, the doorbell rang.

She gave herself one last critical glance, decided it would have to do, then went to the front door. Her heart pounded in her chest and her pulse throbbed in her temples as she peered through the peephole and saw Ken standing there. She didn't know what was getting into her; she hadn't been this nervous before a date since her first boyfriend in college.

After getting a look at Ken, she had to rest her forehead against the door and take a couple of deep breaths before she could open it. He wore a dove-gray suit that she knew would do wonderful things for his eyes. This was going to be one wedding where she didn't have to worry as much about her date's romantic thoughts as she did her own. It was going to take every ounce of her self-control to keep from fantasizing all sorts of romantic things about him.

When she felt she could face him without leaping into his arms, Jenny opened the door and greeted him with a smile. "Hi!" she said. It was all she could think of to say as she got lost in his eyes. She had been right—that suit did some pretty wonderful things to his gray eyes.

"Hi," he said in return. "You look nice."

"Thank you." When she could tear herself away from his eyes, she said, "Let me get my purse, and we can go." She was halfway down the hallway to get to her purse before she realized she'd forgotten to invite him inside. There went several hours of cleaning, wasted. She grabbed her purse and hurried back to the door. "I should have asked you in. Sorry," she said, not sure what else she could say about such an obvious lapse in manners. This date was off to a fine start. Good thing she wasn't really trying to make an impression.

Ken escorted her to his car and helped her inside. Once he was in his seat, he said, "Okay, point the way." She directed him toward the church, glad of the chance to give him directions. Otherwise she wouldn't have known what to say. That was the downside of the long conversation she'd had with him the night they met. She knew too much about him. There wasn't much else to ask.

"How have you been doing?" he asked when she finished directing him to their destination.

"Pretty well. Nothing exciting to report. And you?" She couldn't believe they were making such banal small talk.

"I'm doing okay, I guess. My mom has asked after you."

Her attention perked up. "Really? How disappointed is she that you haven't brought me around again?"

"I've been so busy with work that I've had plenty of excuses not to visit, so she doesn't know that you're not a permanent addition."

"Oh," Jenny said. She wasn't sure if that was good or bad news.

He pulled into the church parking lot. "I guess this is the place," he said. "Before we go in, is there anything about this group I need to know?"

She shook her head. "Not really. Just what I told you on the phone. No one is expecting a boyfriend. These are just my friends from church. You could even tell the truth, that you're just a friend I asked to come with me, although I'd appreciate it if you didn't bring up the fact that we met in a bar."

"Your wish is my command," he said with a slight bow toward her. He wasn't smiling, though. She wondered what was wrong.

He got out of the car and opened her door for her, then offered his elbow to escort her into the chapel. They took a seat on the bride's side of the church, then sat quietly as the organist played a number of familiar Bach selections.

Jenny stole a glance at Ken. He was staring at the front of the chapel, his jaw clenched and his eyes steely. She knew she'd been far too flaky today, out of sheer nerves, but she didn't think her behavior could have been enough to set him off like this. Then she remembered how she met him—after the last wedding he'd gone to. She wanted to kick herself. Of all the things for her to invite him to, a wedding wasn't the best idea. Poor guy, she was forcing him to relive one of the worst nights of his life. It would have been better for her to decline the invitation or to go alone. But it had felt so good to have someone to invite, for a change.

She gingerly touched his elbow and whispered, "Ken?" He turned to look at her. "I'm so sorry, Ken. I completely forgot. I shouldn't have put you through this."

His eyebrows quirked upward and he opened his mouth to say something, but the organist struck up Pachelbel's Canon and the bridesmaids began to glide down the aisle. Jenny turned to watch. As content as she was to be single at this time in her life, the little girl in her thrilled to the pageantry of a wedding. It probably had more to do with childhood games of putting scarves over her head and walking down the hallway in her white nightgown than with any longing to walk down the aisle herself, but she got goose bumps when the doors at the back of the chapel were flung open and the bride appeared.

After the bride made her way down the aisle and the minister had seated the guests, Jenny glanced at Ken again. Seeing the bride come down the aisle had probably been the most difficult thing for him, for that was when he said he'd realized his feelings for Kristen. He didn't seem to be suffering too much now, but his stone-like face could be hiding it.

She settled back to watch the ceremony. This was the easy part of a wedding for her. All she had to do was sit there. It was the reception she dreaded. Maybe she could have spared Ken some pain by suggesting he meet her at the reception rather than making him sit through the ceremony.

The sensation of his shoulder pressed against hers was enough to distract her from the ceremony. She glanced at him to find him looking at her instead of toward the altar. Her face burning, she quickly looked away again. She'd hate for him to think she was being inspired to romantic thoughts by a wedding. That would be the surest way to scare him away, and it would contradict everything she'd said before. Resolving not to let herself become distracted again, she returned her attention to the front of the church and tried to ignore the warmth of his shoulder against hers.

Maybe he was just a hopeless romantic. That was the only explanation Ken could think of for the way weddings affected him. The last time he had watched a bride walk down the aisle, he had been sure his life was over because she wasn't his bride. Now every time he glanced at Jenny, he saw her wearing white and gazing up at him with love in her eyes. Even that funny little glare she'd given him hadn't been enough to throw cold water on his fantasy. He really needed to get over this, he thought.

Not that Jenny hadn't given him plenty of other reasons not to indulge in wedding fantasies about her. The number of times she'd managed to slip it into the conversation that he was just a friend she was bringing to the wedding was a pretty good clue.

But that didn't mean he didn't get a pang of longing when the bride and groom kissed and turned to face the wedding guests as man and wife. He chanced one more glance at Jenny and saw a slight smile on her lips. Maybe things weren't so bleak, after all. Then he realized what he was thinking and tried to snap out of it. *Remember what you promised yourself*, he told himself mentally. He was here today to help Jenny's social life so she wouldn't need a stand-by date again, not to lose his heart. He could hardly wait to get to the reception to put his plan in motion.

* * *

The reception was being held in the same hotel where they'd first met—after the last reception Ken had attended. Fortunately, this one was in a different ballroom.

After turning the car over to the hotel valets, they found the ballroom where the reception was being held. A small jazz combo in a corner of the room provided upbeat background music. The tiny dance floor remained empty as the guests concentrated on the buffet tables. A champagne fountain spouted a sparkling punch, and waiters circled the room, offering glasses to the assembled guests.

Jenny glanced nervously around her as they waited their turn to sign the guest book. "I feel like I'm trapped in Noah's Ark here," she whispered to Ken. "Everyone's here two by two."

Ken looked around and realized she was right. Almost everyone in the room was part of a couple. He'd never thought of it before, but he'd always gone to weddings with a date, until the last one, and he remembered how difficult that one had been.

"Okay, I see your point," he admitted. "I wouldn't want to be here alone. Aren't you glad you have me?"

She jabbed him in the ribs with her elbow as she finished signing her name in the guest book. "Don't get full of yourself," she warned.

They found seats at a table near the periphery of the room, away from the dance floor. "I'll get us some punch," Ken offered, then slipped away into the crowd. With any luck, someone else had noticed them come in together. Maybe the fact that Jenny was with someone her friends didn't know might spark some interest in one of her male friends. There was nothing like seeing a woman with another man to make a man realize what she meant to him. He ought to know.

He filled two glasses with punch and started to head back to the table, but paused when he saw a man approach Jenny. His plan was already working.

Ken hadn't been gone long when Jenny noticed the man seated at a nearby table. It was ex-boyfriend number three, the most recent one, who had been far more interested in her than she was in him. With any luck, he was still too annoyed with her to speak to her. She edged her chair around so she wouldn't risk making eye contact with him. This was why it was getting harder to find good stand-by dates as she got older. Everyone she knew that she might be willing to go out with, she had already dated, and there was usually a good reason they weren't dating anymore.

She scanned the room, looking for her friends and wondering what was taking Ken so long. She didn't see him near the punch bowl, but she did see someone else she recognized. His name was Steve, and he was another ex-boyfriend, the jerk who hadn't had the guts to actually break up with her. He'd just quit calling, then had acted as if nothing had ever happened between them the next time she'd seen him. He was also the last man she'd allowed herself to develop any deep feelings for.

She glanced away quickly, but it was too late. He'd looked up just in time to see her and make eye contact with her. And worse, he was heading straight for her. If she'd been near a window, she would have been tempted to throw herself through it. But she wasn't, so she could either crawl under the table or face him.

She decided facing him was the least embarrassing option. "Hi, Jenny!" he said as he approached her. "You look great."

She forced herself to smile up at him and fought back

the urge to kick him in the shins. "Thanks," she said. "It's been a while."

He was the one to break eye contact with her. "Yeah, I know. You wouldn't believe how busy I've been." He was right. She probably wouldn't, mostly because it wasn't true.

"Oh, I can imagine," she said, craning her neck to look for Ken. Where had he gone? This was when she needed her date nearby, and he was out of sight.

Steve continued smiling his oily grin. She would have loved to slap it off his face, but she decided to take the high road. He'd hurt her, but she didn't want him to know it.

"Wouldn't you know, they ran out just as I got to the front of the line."

Jenny struggled to suppress her relieved grin when she heard Ken's voice. She accepted the punch cup he held out to her, then squeezed his hand in thanks as she smiled up at him. "I was wondering what happened to you," she said.

She noticed that Ken was glaring at Steve. Not wanting to give him the wrong impression, she hurried to make introductions. "Steve, this is Ken. Ken, Steve is an old friend." Two could play at that faulty memory game, she thought. Then to make sure Steve got the picture, she held on to Ken's hand and gazed up at him with an expression that ought to make it quite clear that Ken was more than an old friend.

Steve cleared his throat. "Well, it was great seeing you again. We'll have to catch up later." He made a quick exit, and Jenny groaned.

"What is it?" Ken asked, taking the seat next to her.

"Oh, nothing." She drank the whole cup of punch in one swallow. It was a small glass, so that wasn't a great feat. A glance across the room told her Steve was still watching her. "Let's dance," she said to Ken.

He looked at her with a quizzical expression, but he stood and extended a hand to help her up, then led her to the dance floor. Only a few other couples were dancing to a slow, romantic number. Ken placed his hand on her back, and she stepped forward to lean against him. "Remind me again what I'm missing about slow dancing," she murmured to him.

He held her a little tighter and began moving them around the dance floor. She closed her eyes and let her body relax against his. This suit wasn't as scratchy against her cheek as the tuxedo had been, and the noisy wedding reception wasn't nearly as intimate as the almost deserted hotel lounge, but the sensation of dancing in his arms was just as good as she remembered.

When the song ended, she stayed close to him and slipped an arm around his waist. His eyes widened in surprise and confusion, but he put an arm around her shoulders to walk her back to their table. Once they had taken their seats, he leaned closer to her and whispered, "Would you mind telling me what that was all about?"

"Have you ever had a nightmare in which you're surrounded by all your ex-girlfriends?"

He frowned. "I may have, but not that I recall."

"Well, it's happening to me now—only it's ex-boyfriends I'm surrounded by. I have got to find a new group of friends so I can quit running into these people."

"I take it that Steve is one of those exes."

"And the worst. The most annoying thing about him is that every time I see him, he conveniently manages to forget we were ever anything more than friends or that he was the one to dump me. I guess I'm supposed to fall at his feet in gratitude that he's still willing to associate with me."

He nodded. "I believe you told me about him. So, you want to make sure he's aware that he's not being missed?"

"If you don't mind?" She felt bad about using Ken for such a purpose, but that was exactly what she needed to put the old relationship behind her.

He smiled. "That's what I'm here for." Edging his chair closer to hers, he put his hand on her back and gently rubbed it. The sensation almost made her leap through her skin. It was probably just the silky material of her dress that had that effect on her, she rationalized. She had to give Ken credit for realism. He even had that heavy-lidded bedroom look just right. No one who happened to look at them would doubt what they'd be doing as soon as they got away from the reception.

The thought was enough to make her giggle, for she knew how wrong they'd be.

"Normally that doesn't induce giggles," Ken intoned in a voice to match his expression.

"I'm sorry," she said, fighting to straighten her face. "But I just couldn't help but think how much of a wrong impression we're giving people. And I'm sorry to make you do this, after I promised you I wouldn't need you to act like a boyfriend."

"It's only fitting, considering the act I needed you to play for me. Think your ex is jealous enough?"

"Probably. But I'm not as worried about making him jealous as I am making sure he knows my life has gone on without him."

"And has it?"

She laughed, "Oh my, yes! I must admit I was a bit blue for a while, mainly because I had no sense of closure. Then I let myself get involved with the next guy to come around, just to prove to myself it was over. But it's been ages since I even thought of Steve. I guess it goes back to my theory that there's a conspiracy against single people. If I'd been on my own when I ran into him, no matter how I felt about the situation, he and others would think I was still hurting over him because I was alone."

"I'm starting to see your point. That was how I felt at my parents' barbecue."

She grinned at him. "I don't sound quite so paranoid anymore, do I?"

He squeezed her shoulder. "You never sounded paranoid."

A round of applause from the wedding guests interrupted their conversation. The bride and groom had finally arrived after completing their photos at the church. The ritual cutting of the wedding cake followed, then the band struck up another dance.

Jenny watched the traditional wedding activities, then turned back to Ken. "I never sounded paranoid to you?" she asked, picking up where their conversation had left off.

"Well, maybe just a little. But you did have a point. It's not easy to be single in this world."

"What's the longest you've gone without being part of a couple?" she asked, leaning forward and resting her chin in her hand.

He frowned, cocked his head to one side, then said, "About a year. The past year, as a matter of fact. Although I have been dating people, off and on, since then."

Her eyebrows rose. "A year? That's all? You must be one of those men who just strings a woman along.

You go out every so often, but the relationship doesn't really progress. And when that one finally dies of starvation, there's usually someone else waiting in the wings."

"Ouch," he said with a wince. "But you may be right about that. That's probably why Kristen is married to someone else now."

"You really don't know what it is to be truly single, to not know who you're going out with next weekend, to not automatically know who you'll invite to the company party or your friend's wedding."

"This is a first," he admitted. "But while we're analyzing these things, how long has it been since you were part of a couple?"

"More than two years," she admitted ruefully. "Give or take a few months. That was with Steve, and it's hard to tell when the relationship actually ended. It depends on whether you count the last time we went out together, the last time he called me or the day I finally gave up on him and realized he wasn't going to call."

"No one since then?"

She shook her head. "No one seriously. I told you about them, the revenge guy and the one I wasn't really interested in. Just a few dates here and there, and I wouldn't have invited either of them to go with me to a wedding. It's pathetic, isn't it?"

"Is there a reason you haven't become involved with anyone since then?"

She laughed. "I haven't found anyone I wanted to be involved with." Shaking a finger at him, she scolded, "I know what you're trying for. You think I'm avoiding getting involved. I guess I am, in a way, but mainly because I'm a lot pickier about who I choose."

"Speaking of the people you choose, there's someone a couple of tables over staring at us."

She sneaked a look, then chuckled. "Yep, another old boyfriend. That one never got very serious, at least, not on my part. It took me a while to convince him that I wasn't going to fall desperately in love with him, but most of that was on the phone. Not too many real dates."

"Ah, yes, you mentioned him. You've just left a trail of broken hearts behind you, haven't you?"

"It's not as bad as it sounds. It's just that they're all here in the same room with me. I told you this was a nightmare."

"Well, we might as well give them something to look at. Let's dance again." He led her to the dance floor and took her into his arms. This time, she didn't have to press herself against him, for he pulled her close as soon as he got his arms around her. The music was soft and slow, with a subtle beat. As they danced, Ken rubbed her back gently. She knew it was just for show, but his touch stirred a deep longing in the pit of her stomach. It had been so long since she'd felt this way about a man. Why did it have to happen now, when the act would end as soon as they left this place?

6

Ken settled his arms around Jenny and tried to get used to the feel of her in his embrace. They'd danced together the night they met, but as strangers, it hadn't felt so awkward. Now that he knew her, he couldn't help being aware of every touch, every move. It felt surprisingly good.

He could feel her gentle curves beneath the flowing fabric of her silky dress. Before today, he never would have believed a floaty, Victorian-looking floral dress could be so alluring, but now he knew better. The song ended, and he was reluctant to let go of her. He looked around the room, hoping he could point out that one of her ex-boyfriends was watching, but they weren't to be found. Reluctantly, he loosened his hold on her and stepped back. "Want to get some cake?" he asked.

She shrugged. "Might as well." He took her elbow and guided her to the table where the wedding cake was being served. Now that they had quit dancing, she edged away from him, keeping a bit of distance between their bodies. His heartbeat stabilized somewhat when she did so. At the cake table, he handed her a plate of cake, and she took it from him with a soft "Thank you." She focused her attention on the cake, as if the confection were absolutely enthralling.

The sudden bout of shyness confused him a bit, but he was feeling the same thing. To avoid increasing the level of awkwardness he took a piece of cake for himself just so he'd have something to do other than talk. He'd barely taken one bite when a shout from behind him almost made him choke.

"Jenny!" He turned to see a pair of women barreling toward them.

Jenny saw them and burst into a grin. "I was wondering if you two were going to be here," she said.

"I haven't seen you in ages," the taller of the two newcomers said.

"Well, I've been busy, I guess. And you have, too," Jenny replied. "How have you been?"

In response, the woman waggled her left hand in front of Jenny's face. The other woman leaned over and said, "Isn't it gorgeous!"

Ken tried to think of a way to make a graceful temporary exit before he got stuck in the middle of some heavy-duty girl talk. He touched Jenny on the elbow and said, "I'll go get us some more punch."

She gasped. "Oh, I'm sorry, I've been so rude. Sharon, Amy, this is Ken. Ken, I'd like you to meet my friends Sharon and Amy."

Sharon, the one with the new engagement ring, looked up at Ken and gave Jenny a sly wink. "Jenny! I'm shocked at you," she said. "Where have you been hiding him?"

"Now we know why we haven't seen her in a while," Amy said. She turned to Ken and said, "You go ahead and get the punch. We're going to be talking about you."

Jenny rolled her eyes and laughed. "It's okay, Ken. I won't tell them anything," she said.

"I'll get the punch," he said. He didn't want to deprive Jenny of the fun of hearing her friends gush over what they thought was her boyfriend. She deserved a little moment of glory. Playing his part in the game, he gave Jenny a quick kiss on the cheek before saying, "I'll be back soon, sweetheart." She rewarded him with a pink flush on her cheeks. He hoped it wasn't because of anger for what he'd presumed to say. She might not want her friends to think she had a serious boyfriend.

As he picked up two cups of punch, he saw Jenny and her friends moving to a table where two men sat. He could see how Jenny would have felt uncomfortable if she were the only member of her group without a date. It wasn't anything her friends did on purpose, but it was difficult for couples to maintain friendships with singles. He'd noticed that he'd seen less of his friends when he and Kristen broke up.

He carried the punch over to where Jenny sat with her friends, where he was introduced to Amy and Sharon's significant others, Jack and Craig—although he wasn't sure which was which. Settling into a chair next to Jenny, he put an arm around her shoulders and she leaned against him. He enjoyed the feel of her next to him. It felt natural, comfortable. It had been a long time since he'd been this way with a woman—none of the edginess of a couple that had just started seeing each other, just the comfort of two people who knew each other well.

Before his imagination ran away from him, he reminded himself that he'd given up the head-over-heels behavior. Jenny was a nice, pretty young woman, and he enjoyed her company. That was all there needed to be. He definitely wasn't planning to go falling in love anytime soon.

The wedding photographer came by the table and said, "Okay, ladies, we're about to toss the bouquet. Everyone get out there."

Sharon winked at her fiancé. "I don't know that I need to get out there, but I figure I'll just seal this up."

"Come on, Jenny," Amy said, "I have a good feeling for you here."

Jenny turned to look at Ken. "Don't worry, I can't catch," she whispered before allowing her friends to lead her to the middle of the floor.

The bouquet went sailing over the heads of all the single women gathered in the middle of the dance floor. Ken noticed that Jenny didn't even reach for it. Sharon snagged it out of the air and held it above her head like a trophy.

"Okay, guys, it's your turn!" the photographer shouted.

Ken joined the young men on the floor. When the garter flew toward him, he easily reached up and grabbed it. It was a couple of seconds before he realized what he'd done. He looked around and saw Jenny staring at him, open-mouthed, from the edge of the dance floor. Her friends elbowed her in the side and gave her congratulatory claps on the shoulder.

The photographer took a picture of Ken with the groom, then said, "Now, who's the lucky young lady?"

Jenny's friends shoved her forward. "Okay, now, show her the garter," the photographer instructed, snapping shots. "Why don't you give her a kiss."

Why not? Ken thought. He bent forward and kissed Jenny on the lips. He'd forgotten how soft and warm they were, so he kissed her just a little more. Whistles and shouts from nearby brought him back to where he was, and he stepped away to see Jenny blushing bright red and staring at the floor.

"Now the lady who caught the bouquet needs to have a dance with the gentleman who caught the garter," the photographer instructed. Ken would have loved to punch him in the teeth, just to shut him up, but he didn't feel he had a choice other than to play along.

Sharon handed the bouquet to her fiancé, then took Ken's hand. The others cheered as the music began, and they danced at arm's length, like two kids in a school dance class. "I'm surprised I haven't heard anything about you from Jenny," Sharon said.

"Well, you know Jenny," Ken said, hoping not to give too much away.

Sharon rolled her eyes. "Yeah, I know. She's really careful about relationships. She's been hurt a few times." She looked him squarely in the eyes. "Jenny's a special person. We don't like seeing her hurt."

"I won't hurt her," he promised, meaning every word of it. He'd do everything he could to keep her from being hurt, even playing the dashing suitor in front of her friends. He had no desire ever to see those green eyes filled with tears again, and he never wanted to be the cause of tears for her.

"Good," she said with a nod. "It's about time she found a decent man. I thought I'd found the last one."

"There are still a few of us left."

The music came to an end, and Ken returned to Jenny. "Did you have to do that?" she whispered when he got close to her.

"I'm sorry. It was just an instinct. And it's just a silly superstition. Don't worry about it. Besides, your ex-boyfriends all got to see that kiss."

She turned even pinker. "What did Sharon have to say out there?"

"She said I'd better be nice to you."

Jenny laughed. "That's Sharon for you."

The band started another song. "What do you say we dance another dance?" he said.

She shook her head. "I don't think so. Unless you really want to stay much longer, why don't we go through the receiving line and get out of here?"

He would have been perfectly willing to let the evening last a while longer, but he didn't think pushing her would be a good idea right now. They said farewell to Jenny's friends, shook hands with the happy couple and their parents, then left the ballroom. As they passed the lobby lounge, Ken leaned closer to Jenny and said, "Want to stop for a drink, for old time's sake?"

She glanced at the lounge, then back at him and shook her head. "Not tonight."

He nodded, and they passed the bar to go to the valet parking stand.

The valet retrieved the car, and as soon as Ken tipped him and took his seat, Jenny turned on him. "Just what did you think you were doing back there?"

"Which part? The garter or the kiss?"

"All of the above. Thank you for helping me put Steve in his place, but the rest of it wasn't necessary."

"And I was just trying to help. You did point out that you were surrounded by ex-boyfriends, and you did say you wouldn't mind making them jealous."

"I know. But now I'm afraid you've got me in big trouble with my friends. They're going to be asking questions about the new boyfriend who appeared from out of the blue to catch the garter, and they're going to wonder what's going on if they don't see you again."

He hadn't thought of that. He concentrated on navigating the one-way downtown streets while he tried to put his thoughts into words. "I'm sorry," he said at last. "But I realized that what you've been saying all along is true, how everyone was paired off, and I could see how you'd been left out because of it. So I thought I'd help."

She shook her head and frowned. "Does that mean you felt sorry for me?"

"No!" he hurried to explain. "But I did feel badly for you. I just thought I'd give you a little boost." He shrugged sheepishly. "Okay, so maybe I overdid it a little."

She raised her eyebrows at him, but he relaxed when he saw the corners of her mouth twitching into a smile. "A little?" she asked. "You were calling me 'sweetheart.' I could feel my teeth decaying on the spot from all that sweetness."

"Yeah, I definitely overdid it," he said with a sheepish grin. He shrugged. "Sorry."

She chuckled, and he finally relaxed. "But I have to admit, it worked. I just never again want to run into that many old boyfriends in one place. I'm glad you were there to come to my rescue."

"Just doing my job, ma'am."

"You did it well. Almost too well. I'll never hear the end of it from Sharon and Amy. But thank you, anyway. At least you meant well."

"Any time. And I mean that. The next time you need a fake boyfriend, give me a call. I'll even help if your friends give you trouble about me." He pulled up in front of her house, helped her out of the car, then walked her to the front door. She hesitated a second, then said, "Would you like to come in?"

He started to accept, but then he remembered putting his arms around her and feeling the body that lay beneath that floaty dress. He wouldn't mind doing that again, but he had a feeling it didn't fit within the definition of a stand-by date, and he didn't want to raise her ire again tonight. It was better if he didn't go anywhere near the temptation. "No, thanks, I'd better get going," he said. "But I meant what I said. Call me if you need me."

"I think I'm the one who owes you now. Let me know if you need an emergency stand-by sometime."

"Don't worry, I will." He started to head down the walk. On impulse, he turned back to kiss her. His original intention was to kiss her on the cheek, but she turned her head just in time for his lips to land on hers. It took every ounce of willpower he had to limit himself to a quick peck rather than a deep kiss. But he didn't want to scare her. As resilient as she appeared, he knew she was fragile underneath, and he knew how weak he could be when it came to women.

"Good night, Jenny," he said, then turned and hurried down the walk before he lost his resolve.

Jenny didn't expect Ken to call her again, not after the way she'd behaved at the wedding. All her good intentions, witty conversational topics and social skills had flown out the window the moment she saw him. The strange reunion of ex-boyfriends hadn't helped matters. Ken was probably convinced she was totally crazy, and she was afraid he was right.

When her phone rang almost a week after the wedding, she nearly dropped it upon hearing Ken's voice. "Uh, hi," she managed to stammer, once more losing her composure.

"It's stand-by date time again, if you're free," he said. "And this time it's not just a generic date. You were invited specifically."

She groaned. "Oh no, your mother!"

"How did you guess? Yep, Mom said I should invite you for Sunday lunch."

"She doesn't think we're still seeing each other, does she?"

There was a little pause from his end of the line. "Well, we are, I guess. We saw each other just last weekend. And honestly, the subject never came up. She just called me out of the blue last night and said I should invite you to lunch. If I'd told her we'd broken up, she wouldn't believe me because she hadn't heard anything about it yet."

"Maybe we shouldn't have been so convincing at the picnic," Jenny said. Not only would they have managed to avoid this trouble, but she would have slept a lot better over the past few weeks. His parents weren't the only ones who'd found that kiss convincing.

"There's nothing to worry about. Just come have some fried chicken, talk a little bit, and she'll be happy. She won't try to embarrass you. You won't even have to worry about Dad's cooking this time. He's forbidden to touch Sunday dinner. And I promise to sneak in on Saturday and hide all the baby pictures, so you won't be forced to look at them and admire how cute I was."

She had to smile at the mental image that inspired. "Oh, I don't know. I don't think I'd mind seeing your baby pictures. It certainly would give me a bit of an advantage over you next time you need me as a stand-by date. I wonder if she'd let me take one, just to have handy at an office party, or a friend's wedding." Jenny was starting to enjoy this, now that she'd managed to relax a bit.

"*I* would mind. Unless you're willing to share your own. Hasn't your mom asked about me?"

"She's not that curious." Not after Jenny had told her the full story, that he only needed a date to show off in front of his old girlfriend. A date that had limited expectations. Her mother didn't even know Ken had accompanied her to the wedding. "She figured you were just a loser," she added, glad he couldn't see her wicked smile.

"She did not. She said I sounded like a nice young man, and it was about time one noticed her daughter," he said with an indignant huff that soon dissolved into a low chuckle. "So, what do you say, Jen? Will you do it? After this, I promise to call her to mope about you breaking up with me so you don't have to do this again. And I'll still blame her for scaring you."

"Can I be there to hear the moping?" she asked.

"You drive a hard bargain. Yes, you can listen to me wallowing in misery."

"Okay, Sunday it is."

"Great! My parents don't live too far from you. They won't be at the lake this weekend. Are you home from church by one?"

"Usually."

"Okay, I'll be by around one. Save room for dessert."

She hung up the phone with a smile, her mood lightened. Then she frowned. She'd never thought of including lunches with parents within the definition of a stand-by date. That was normally something she didn't subject herself to unless she was really serious about a man. But this whole stand-by date relationship had broken all her rules so far. Why should it stop now?

* * *

The Parkses' usual home was even more impressive than the lake house, although not very ostentatious. Jenny had to wonder again how Ken had managed to stay single in this town, with his looks and charm, and money on top of it. She would have thought women would come all the way from Dallas just for the chance to snag him.

Then she remembered. He was still single because at a crucial juncture, he had made that choice. She couldn't help wondering if he really did have some kind of commitment problem. He seemed the type who would have trouble settling on just one woman on a permanent basis.

Ken's mother, dressed in Sunday best rather than lake wear, was just as friendly and casual as Jenny remembered and greeted her with a big hug. "I'm so glad you could come. I've been wondering why Ken hasn't brought you back. I guess he's been keeping you all to himself."

Jenny felt her cheeks grow warm. She glanced at Ken to see him roll his eyes. "I was afraid you'd terrify her away from me, Mom," he said. "After the picnic, I had to beg her to see me again."

Ellen Parks faced her son, her hands on her hips, and said, "Kenneth Parks! Don't you lie to your mother like that." She turned to Jenny and said, "That isn't true at all, now is it?"

"Well..." Jenny began, but Ken cut her off.

"Why don't we go distract Dad while you finish up with lunch. I take it you've managed to keep him away?"

"I threw the sports section from the Sunday paper at him. He's been otherwise occupied. But you'd be proud of your father. I've been teaching him a little at a time, and this week he managed a casserole that didn't make anyone ill." She winked at Jenny. "It didn't taste great, but at least it wasn't deadly."

Jenny laughed, feeling at ease with the good-natured family banter. It wouldn't be too difficult to fit in with this family, even if she really was Ken's girlfriend. "Do you need any help from me?" she offered. "I'm probably as bad as Mr. Parks in the kitchen, but I'm willing to help."

Ellen raised her eyebrows, smiled, then glanced at her son, as if for approval. Ken gave a deep sigh, then nodded. "Okay, you two can go into the kitchen and talk about me. I'll get Dad to help set the table."

Jenny handed her purse to Ken, then followed Ellen into the kitchen. As soon as they were out of earshot of the men, Ellen grinned. "I'm going to let you in on a little secret," she said. "I'm cooking in the microwave today. It was all done ahead." With a wink, she added, "But I'd appreciate it if you wouldn't tell anyone. I get treated a lot better if it seems I've been slaving over a hot stove."

"Your secret's safe with me," Jenny assured her. "I honestly don't know how people survived without microwaves. I'd starve without mine."

Ellen opened the refrigerator door and started handing dishes to Jenny. "I bought one almost as soon as they came out," she said, her head still inside the refrigerator. "They were huge and ugly, but it sure beat cooking." She straightened and shut the door. "Okay, those two go in for five minutes at high power," she said, taking the rest of the dishes from Jenny, who put the two dishes she still held into the microwave and set the timer.

"I'm afraid I've given my son unrealistic expectations for a wife," Ellen continued. "He just remembers home-cooked meals with the whole family around the table.

He doesn't remember that I used the microwave more often than the stove." She gave Jenny a measuring glance and said, "I don't know if that's something you need to worry about or not, but I thought I'd warn you."

Jenny couldn't look her in the eye. She had already come to like Ellen, and she hated to disappoint her. She also hated to get Ken into a difficult situation. "If Ken's expecting home-cooked meals every night from his wife, he's going to be terribly disappointed," she said. Ellen could decide for herself how to apply the remark. Jenny felt it was a safe enough statement to make about any modern woman with a career.

"I hope he will be. Disappointed, that is. He can learn to cook his own meals. It may have taken almost forty years of marriage, but his father managed. Not that Ken's helpless," she hurried to add, probably out of fear of selling her son short. "He has been on his own for quite a while."

The microwave timer went off, and Ellen said, "You can take those dishes out and put these other two in, for the same amount of time. Then we'll just put the first two into serving dishes, and we'll throw a couple of pots into the sink so it looks like we worked harder."

Jenny laughed. "Do they really believe it?"

"If they haven't figured it out by now, I'm concerned about their intelligence, but until someone says something, it's kind of fun to play along." While Jenny worked with the microwave, Ellen turned on the oven and slid in a pan of brown-and-serve rolls.

"So, how are things going with you and Ken? Anything in the works?"

Jenny almost dropped the serving dish she held. "Oh, things are going okay, I guess," she said, not quite sure what to say.

"Okay? That's it? Is something wrong?"

"Well, we haven't been going out all that long, and we're both busy, so we don't see a lot of each other," Jenny said, focusing on putting the vegetables into serving dishes so she wouldn't have to look Ellen in the eye. "So it's really too early to say how things are going."

"Let me guess. 'Too busy' means he gets so caught up in his work that he forgets to call you."

Jenny didn't know how to answer that one. If Ken had meant what he said about telling his mother later that they were breaking up, then she could set the stage now. But she could also set the stage for a difficult mother/son conversation if she wasn't careful. "I'm the one who's busy," she said, opting out of having to make a choice. "I can be really hard to reach. And my job sometimes keeps me busy on weekends."

"Okay. But don't you let him ignore you. I don't want him to mess around and lose you." She didn't say it, but Jenny heard the implied completion of the sentence: "...like he lost Kristen."

Snapping out of her solemn mood, Ellen said, "Why don't you take those dishes out to the dining room. It's through that door. I'll finish up in here."

Grateful for the chance to escape the kitchen, Jenny picked up the two serving dishes and went through the door Ellen had indicated. Inside the dining room, Ken and his father were arranging silverware on the table. Jenny set the dishes on trivets on the table, then said, "Need any help from me?"

"I think we've just about got it under control," Ken said, "but you're welcome to supervise."

Ellen joined them a moment later, bearing the last of

the dishes. "Dinner is served!" she announced with a flourish. "Jenny, you can sit there, across from Ken."

Jenny took her seat as the others moved to what seemed to be their accustomed spots. Glancing across the table at Ken, Jenny had to look away quickly to avoid bursting into a fit of giggles. He had rolled his eyes at her and winked and she had a feeling he knew exactly what his mother had said to her in the kitchen.

Jenny reminded herself that it really didn't matter what his parents thought of her, since she was going to "break up" with him soon. And she could understand that his mother wouldn't have bought an abrupt breakup earlier. Ellen Parks would have dragged the two of them together and attempted couples counseling on her own.

Still, Jenny maintained her best manners and responded politely to all queries about herself. After all, she'd kind of like Ken's parents to be a little upset that she broke up with him.

She was lucky that Ken's father didn't say much, kept his questions carefully neutral, and managed to change the subject when Ellen pried too deeply. Even so, by the time she finished her dessert, Jenny felt as if she'd been interrogated by the Gestapo. She hadn't had to discuss her third-grade teacher, but that was about the only stone of her life left unturned, or so it seemed.

She could have hugged Ken when he announced right after dinner that they had someplace else to go. They thanked his parents for their hospitality, then made their escape. As soon as they were safely ensconced in Ken's car and on their way, Jenny leaned back in her seat with a deep sigh. "I'm so glad you managed to get us away when you did. I have nothing against your parents, but I can't remember the name of my third-grade teacher, and that's the only thing your mother didn't ask me."

"No problem. I was starting to worry that she'd run out of questions for you and start asking me for updates on my life. I admit, she can be a bit much at times."

"But she is sweet, and she does care about you."

"And someday she'll realize that I've grown up."

"Oh, I think she's very well aware of that fact. That's why she wants to see you happy."

He grinned. "Yeah, I know. And she also wants grandkids to spoil."

Jenny had wondered if he really had plans for someplace else to go, but he seemed to be heading straight back to her house. "I don't know about you," he said, "but my plans for the afternoon include a baseball game on TV while I sift through a mountain of documents. So I was telling the truth about having someplace I needed to be."

She shrugged. "I guess I'll just finish reading the paper." The sting of disappointment she felt came as a surprise. She normally liked to spend Sunday afternoons reading the newspaper. Today, though, she wouldn't have minded doing something else.

They reached her house, and he walked her to the door. "Thanks again," he said. "You've taken a lot of pressure off me. And I promise I'll tell my mom we've broken up before she can invite us for dinner again."

"It wasn't that bad, but I don't want to set up any false hopes for her. Something tells me that if she sees you with a woman more than a few times, she starts shopping for mother-of-the-groom dresses."

He laughed. "I think she's had one in her closet for about three years now. We could decide to get married tonight, and she'd be ready."

Married tonight? That didn't sound like such a bad idea, Jenny thought, looking up at him. Then she blinked and forced reality to return. She wasn't looking for marriage. "I guess it's your turn next," he said, patting her shoulder. "Just give me a call, and I'll be ready." He ambled down the walk without even giving her a kiss on the cheek.

"You'd think I'd learn," Jenny said to herself as she went inside and closed the door behind her. Just because Ken was good-looking and his parents seemed to like her didn't mean he was Mr. Right. She'd dated men with better credentials before, and that had always turned out badly. It would be downright silly of her to let herself get involved with a man she knew from the start would break her heart. He'd said it himself—just when he should have been making a commitment, he'd decided he needed time to think. She didn't need to have that sort of thing happen to her again.

It would probably be a good idea not to call him again until she really needed a date. Better safe than sorry. And better lonely than heartbroken.

7

Jenny's next biggest fear struck when her friend Sharon called her at work Monday afternoon. "I've been planning to call you since I saw you at the wedding last week, but time just got away from me," she said. "I've been trying on wedding gowns to the point I never want to see white satin again."

Jenny was glad to hear from her friend, but she dreaded what she was sure would come next.

Sharon didn't disappoint. "So, you've got to tell me all about Ken. What about lunch tomorrow? I'll call Amy and see if she can join us."

It had been ages since Jenny had gotten together with her friends for a girls' day out. She didn't relish the thought of being grilled about Ken, but she couldn't resist the chance to get caught up with Amy and Sharon. It would be like old times, before men got in the way. "I'm free for lunch tomorrow. Where do we want to meet?"

"Someplace that serves salad. That's one bad thing about white. It makes you look so much bigger."

They decided on a restaurant and set a time to meet for lunch. Now Jenny had less than twenty-four hours to get her story together, and knowing her friends, she'd better have it down cold.

* * *

She'd barely taken her seat and unfolded her napkin the next day when the interrogation began.

"Okay, spill the details about Ken," Sharon said. "He's gorgeous, and seems like a really nice guy."

"He is," Jenny assured her. And he was. That was no lie. He just wasn't what she needed in a relationship right now.

"Well?" Sharon leaned forward and raised her eyebrows.

"Well, what?"

"How did you two hook up? How long has it been going on? How serious does it look? Details, Jen, we want details. Don't keep us in suspense."

Jenny didn't want to share the true story of their meeting, so she kept it vague and tried to work in a little damage control. "We just got started talking and went on from there. We've only known each other about a couple of months. And we're really just friends. It's not grown to the heavy romance stage yet."

Sharon and Amy exchanged glances, then Amy said, "Friends? I saw the way you two were at the wedding. You just about melted the ice sculptures with that kiss, not to mention the way you were on the dance floor." She fanned herself with her napkin to emphasize her point.

"And he called you *sweetheart*," Sharon added. "That was so cute. He really likes you. I can tell."

"You think so?"

"I'm sure of it. What do you think, Amy?"

Amy nodded. "Yep. The boy's definitely got it bad for you. And I've got a sense for these kinds of things."

Jenny tried to fight back the unreasonable hope that rose in her heart at her friends' words. What was she thinking? She didn't want Ken to be crazy about her. He was supposed to be her safe date. A man ceased to be a safe date when he "got it bad," as Amy had so quaintly put it.

"It's not that serious," Jenny insisted. "I think the wedding just went to his head. He was never like that before, and he hasn't been since then."

"Has he introduced you to his parents?" Amy asked.

"We had lunch with them Sunday," Jenny had to admit, and she couldn't explain her way out of that one without giving away the whole story.

"Oh, my, it's worse than I thought," Amy breathed, her eyes wide.

"I'll save all my bridal magazines for you," Sharon put in. "Something tells me you'll be needing them. And I want to make it known right now that I refuse to wear a bridesmaid's dress that requires petticoats."

"I met his parents about the same time I met him," Jenny tried to explain before this got out of hand. "It's not like he introduced me to them. They were the ones to invite me over."

"I've never known a man to introduce a woman to his mother unless he was really serious about her," Sharon intoned. "Jack introduced me to his parents one weekend and popped the question the next."

Jenny felt trapped. Everything she said just made things worse, and now it had gone so far, she couldn't tell the real story without looking foolish. She was going to kill Ken for getting her into this, if she ever got together with him again.

Sharon took care of that in her next breath. "Jack and I, and Amy and Craig were all planning on getting together for dinner Friday night. Why don't you and Ken join us? Then we could evaluate him better for you."

Jenny didn't think that was such a good idea. What if

her friends became even more convinced about their hot romance? "I don't know if Ken is free," she hedged. She hated to ask him to do this. Then again, he'd started it, and he said he'd done it to help her be part of the group again. Well, it looked like he'd made himself part of the group, too. He'd just have to deal with it, she decided. "I'll have to ask him."

Sharon gave her hand a squeeze and said, "I'm so glad you're seeing someone. I know we've kind of left you out a bit while we've been caught up in couples things, but now we can really get together as a group again."

"I'll let you know what Ken says."

"Great! I hope he can make it. I've missed spending time with you."

"So have I." Jenny didn't entirely blame her friends for the fact that they'd drifted apart. If she had a boyfriend, she'd want to spend time with him. And she really hated being a fifth wheel, so she was glad they hadn't included her out of pity. She'd turned down the invitations they had offered. But her social life, on the skids since her friends became involved in relationships, was suddenly picking up now that she had been seen in public with Ken. It only reinforced her belief that society discriminated against singles.

That night, she was less nervous about calling Ken than she had been before. If he had subjected her to his mother's questioning, he could survive a night with her chatty friends. At least he'd have the chance to escape a little with Jack and Craig.

When she called, his answering machine picked up. "Hi, it's Jenny," she said after the beep. "Looks like I'll need an escort Friday evening, if you're free. Let me know." She hung up, wondering where he was. Then she dismissed her paranoid worries. He was a lawyer, so he was probably working late. Or maybe he was at the gym. She doubted he'd found another woman to go out with since yesterday afternoon. He didn't seem eager to get involved with anyone, based on the way he was around her. Maybe he was still a safe date, after all.

Ken came home from work and threw his briefcase on the kitchen table. He hadn't planned to stay so late, but he was working against a deadline. He was just about to head to the bedroom when he noticed the light on his answering machine blinking.

When he heard Jenny's voice on the message playback, he smiled, suddenly not feeling quite so tired anymore. Glancing at the clock, he saw that it was close to ten. He wondered if that might be too late to call, but he didn't want to leave her waiting for an answer overnight.

He picked up the phone and dialed her number. She answered on the third ring. "Hi, it's me," he said. "I hope I didn't wake you up or disturb you."

"No, I'm not in bed yet," she said. "I was just getting ready."

Ken couldn't help wondering what she wore to bed. Was it something sensible, like an oversized T-shirt, or perhaps something a little more romantic, like a lace-trimmed nightgown? Or maybe something slinky and silky. An image of her in the last popped into his mind. He shook his head to clear the thought away before saying, "So, you need me Friday night?"

"Yeah. My social life seems to be on the upswing."

"What's the occasion?"

An Important Message from the Editors of Silhouette®

Dear Reader,

Because you've chosen to read one of our fine romance novels, we'd like to say "thank you!" And, as a <u>special</u> way to thank you, we've selected <u>two more</u> of the books you love so well, <u>plus</u> an exciting mystery gift, to send you absolutely **FREE!**

Please enjoy them with our compliments...

Candy Lee

Editor

P.S. And because we <u>value</u> our customers, we've attached something extra inside...

EDITOR'S FREE GIFT SEAL THANK YOU

Peel off seal and Place inside...

How to validate your
Editor's FREE GIFT "Thank You"

1. Peel off gift seal from front cover. Place it in space provided at right. This automatically entitles you to receive two free books and a fabulous mystery gift.

2. Send back this card and you'll get brand-new Silhouette Yours Truly™ novels. These books have a cover price of $3.50 each, but they are yours to keep absolutely free.

3. There's no catch. You're under no obligation to buy anything. We charge nothing—ZERO—for your first shipment. And you don't have to make any minimum number of purchases—not even one!

4. The fact is thousands of readers enjoy receiving books by mail from the Silhouette Reader Service™. They like the convenience of home delivery...they like getting the best new novels BEFORE they're available in stores... and they love our discount prices!

5. We hope that after receiving your free books you'll want to remain a subscriber. But the choice is yours— to continue or cancel, any time at all! So why not take us up on our invitation, with no risk of any kind. You'll be glad you did!

6. Don't forget to detach your FREE BOOKMARK. And remember...just for validating your Editor's Free Gift Offer, we'll send you THREE gifts, *ABSOLUTELY FREE!*

GET A FREE MYSTERY GIFT.

YOURS FREE!

SURPRISE MYSTERY GIFT COULD BE YOURS **FREE** AS A SPECIAL "THANK YOU" FROM THE EDITORS OF SILHOUETTE

The Editor's "Thank You" Free Gifts Include:

- **Two BRAND-NEW romance novels!**
- **An exciting mystery gift!**

PLACE FREE GIFT SEAL HERE

YES! I have placed my Editor's "Thank You" seal in the space provided above. Please send me 2 free books and a fabulous mystery gift. I understand I am under no obligation to purchase any books, as explained on the back and on the opposite page.

201 SDL CF4G (U-SIL-YT-03/98)

Name

Address   Apt.

City

State   Zip

Thank You!

Offer limited to one per household and not valid to current Silhouette Yours Truly™ subscribers. All orders subject to approval.

© 1996 HARLEQUIN ENTERPRISES LTD.   **PRINTED IN U.S.A.**

DETACH AND MAIL CARD TODAY!

The Silhouette Reader Service™ — Here's How It Works:

Accepting free books places you under no obligation to buy anything. You may keep the books and gift and return the shipping statement marked "cancel." If you do not cancel, about a month later we will send you 4 additional novels, and bill you just $2.90 each plus 25¢ delivery per book and applicable sales tax, if any.* That's the complete price, and—compared to cover prices of $3.50 each—quite a bargain! You may cancel at any time, but if you choose to continue, every other month we'll send you 4 more books, which you may either purchase at the discount price...or return to us and cancel your subscription.

*Terms and prices subject to change without notice. Sales tax applicable in N.Y.

If offer card is missing write to: The Silhouette Reader Service, 3010 Walden Ave., P.O. Box 1867, Buffalo, NY 14240-1867

BUSINESS REPLY MAIL
FIRST-CLASS MAIL   PERMIT NO. 717   BUFFALO, NY

POSTAGE WILL BE PAID BY ADDRESSEE

SILHOUETTE READER SERVICE
3010 WALDEN AVE
PO BOX 1867
BUFFALO NY 14240-9952

NO POSTAGE
NECESSARY
IF MAILED
IN THE
UNITED STATES

"It's not really what I'd call an occasion. More like a gathering."

"What kind of gathering would that be?"

"Do you remember my friends Sharon and Amy from the wedding?"

How could he forget? Sharon had practically threatened him with bodily harm if he hurt Jenny. "Sure, I remember them."

"Well, Sharon and her fiancé and Amy and her boyfriend are getting together Friday night for dinner. They've invited us to join them. I know it's not a typical stand-by date, but I wouldn't have been invited along on a couples excursion if it weren't for you, so I can't go without you."

He grinned, glad she couldn't see him. It appeared that his plan had worked. Her social life was improving already. Remembering how she'd reacted to his offer of help, he declined to point out that he'd been right. "I'll be there," was all he said. She'd thank him someday.

"Great. Thank you so much." Her voice sounded relieved. Had she really thought he'd refuse to go?

"Glad to help. And it does sound like fun. Just let me know when and where."

"And I should warn you, they're going to want to know all about you."

"I think I'll be all right. Don't worry. If you survived my parents, I can survive your friends."

She laughed. "We'll see about that."

"If all else fails, you can enjoy watching me squirm."

After he hung up the phone, Ken smiled to himself. He could give Jenny's friends a show they'd be talking about for weeks. Even if he wasn't around, they'd need to schedule a girls' night out just to hash over the couples outing.

And then he'd have to find a way to draw the attention of a nice guy who would be good to her and rescue her from the jerk she was hanging around with.

As she and Ken walked from the remote parking lot to the Stockyards entertainment district, Jenny tried to warn him about her friends. "Sharon can talk a lot, and Amy can get giggly at times, but they're both wonderful friends. Don't let them embarrass you. If you act like they're getting to you, they'll get worse."

"I think I'll be okay. Don't worry."

She shook her head. He had no idea what he was getting himself into. "The two of them together will make your mother look like an amateur. By the time they're through with you, they'll have compiled a dossier that would beat anything the FBI could put together. And worse, you won't even realize they've done it."

He shrugged. "I don't have anything to hide."

She stopped in her tracks. After a couple of steps, he realized she was no longer beside him and turned back to face her. "Yes, you do," she said. "They think you're my boyfriend. They think there's something hot and heavy going on here. No matter how much I try to deny it and say we're just in the friends stage, they don't believe me."

"Then what are you worrying about? Maybe if we don't convince them that we're hot and heavy, they'll believe you about the status of our relationship."

She shook her head, exasperated. "No, you don't get it. What I'm worried about is them finding out what's really going on here. I'll never live it down if they find out you're just a mercy date because I didn't have anyone else to take to that wedding."

"It's okay. I think we've got our story straight. And

if we convinced my parents, we can convince anyone. Besides, they won't be looking for evidence we don't have a relationship. They'll be wanting us to be happy together, and they'll be looking for proof that we will be."

He reached out one arm in a gesture for her to walk toward him, and as she fell into step beside him, he put his arm lightly around her shoulder and gave her a squeeze. She stiffened initially at the contact, but relaxed as she realized how good it felt. He left his arm around her shoulders as they walked, and she silently hoped he wouldn't move it.

As they walked through the Stockyards, past the crowds of tourists and real cowboys in Western wear, she wondered if she was making a wise decision being here tonight. Sooner or later, her friends were going to find out that she and Ken had never been involved. Going through with this charade would only make it worse when the time came.

But there was no backing out now, for her friends were waiting in front of the restaurant at the old train depot. Amy and Sharon ran forward to greet them. "We already put our names on a waiting list for a table," Amy said. "Jack and Craig are inside holding our spots."

"Are we that late?" Jenny asked.

Sharon shook her head. "No. This time Jack set an earlier time to make sure I'd be on time. I surprised him and was ready early." With a quick grin she added, "This marriage may go through after all."

Ken tightened his hold on Jenny's shoulder as Amy and Sharon led them through the Friday-night throng on the sidewalk to the restaurant they'd chosen. They found Jack and Craig leaning against a wall in the vestibule.

"We're fourth on the list," Jack reported, after greeting Ken and Jenny. He had to shout to be heard above the din. The tin ceiling added to the atmosphere of the barbecue restaurant, but didn't help the acoustics.

Jenny was grateful that it was too noisy for conversation in the waiting area. That would give everyone a little less time during the course of the evening to learn too much about Ken. Oblivious to her concerns, Ken moved his arm from her shoulder to her waist, then drew her up against himself and bent to give her a quick kiss on the forehead.

Startled, she looked up at him to see him looking down at her with a smile that made her melt inside. He was one heck of an actor. If he acted like this much longer, she'd have to keep reminding herself that they weren't really a hot item—and she knew the real story. Convincing her friends should be a breeze.

The hostess called out Jack's name and led them to their table. Inside the restaurant, it was a little less noisy, but not quiet enough for intimate conversation. Jenny doubted very many marriage proposals happened in this place. The others stepped aside and let Ken and Jenny slide onto a booth seat together. The other couples took chairs on the other sides of the table. Jenny slid as far as she could to give Ken room, but he moved right next to her, so that their thighs were pressed together underneath the red-checkered vinyl tablecloth.

"Don't overdo it," she warned in a whisper into his ear. Apparently not hearing her, he took advantage of the opportunity to kiss her. She could feel her cheeks turning red. If he kept this up, by the end of the evening her friends not only wouldn't believe her assertion that they were just friends, they'd be expecting a wedding any day now. She dreaded having to tell them eventually that nothing was going to happen. At the rate she and Ken were going with his parents and her friends, they'd have to invent a spectacular breakup when either of them found someone to really date.

The group ordered the family-style barbecue platter, and after the waitress brought their drinks, the interrogation began.

"Ken, Jenny hasn't told us a thing about you. I think she was trying to keep you a secret," Amy began. "Or do you have a dark, mysterious past?" A giggle marred her attempt at an ominous tone.

"I'm afraid I can't tell you that," Ken said, his voice stern, but his eyes laughing. "I'm in the witness protection program, so my identity must remain secret."

Jenny rolled her eyes and gave him a gentle jab in the ribs with her elbow. "What he's afraid to tell you is that he's a lawyer."

Sharon groaned. "Oh Jenny, I thought you knew better. I'm so disappointed."

Shrugging her shoulders and darting a malicious grin at Ken, Jenny said, "Well, it was the best I could do, and I was desperate." Little did they know how true that was.

"Hey!" Ken protested.

"These are my friends, and I can be honest with them," Jenny said sweetly. Best of all, it was the truth.

"I'm guessing it was love at first sight," Sharon said with a dreamy sigh.

Jenny had to fight back a laugh. Her first impression of Ken had been that he was a lounge lizard. Ken surprised her by saying, "Let's just say that the moment I saw her, I knew nothing would be the same for me."

She turned to him in shock, forgetting her friends for a moment. Did he really mean that? As if in answer to her unspoken question, he smiled down at her with a look in his eyes that made her heart skip a beat. Either he was an Oscar-caliber actor, or there just might be something going on here. She wasn't sure what to think about that prospect, so she put it out of her mind before it took hold.

Forcing herself to look away from him, she managed a grin and said, "I don't know that it was love at first sight for me, but I did worry that I might never see him again." She hoped her voice didn't shake too much when she said it, but the restaurant was so noisy that it was difficult to tell if it did.

Sharon squeezed Jack's hand where it rested on top of the table and said, "That's so sweet. We knew it would happen for you eventually. After you've kissed as many frogs as you have, one of them's bound to turn out to be a prince."

"And boy, has she kissed some frogs," Amy said with a wry smile.

"Sharon, how are the wedding plans coming?" Jenny asked, in an attempt to sidetrack the conversation. Ken had met a couple of the frogs, but that didn't mean he needed to hear more about them. She'd discussed her pathetic romantic history during that long conversation in the hotel lounge, but there was no need to remind him of it. His admission that he had felt sorry for her at the wedding still rankled.

"One word of advice," Sharon said with a groan. "Elope. This wedding business is exasperating. It's a good thing we agree on everything, isn't it, dear?" She and Jack nuzzled noses, and Jenny remembered why she had spent so much less time with her friend after she fell in love. It could be unappetizing, being around such a cute couple.

But this time, Ken was there to keep her from feeling like such an outsider. The feel of his hand running gently up and down her arm was enough to distract her from Sharon and Jack's public display of affection. With the way her arm was tingling, and the way that tingle spread throughout her body, Jenny was close to a public display of affection herself. She wondered if Ken had any idea what he was doing to her.

The waitress arrived and placed a platter overflowing with barbecued ribs, sausage, chicken and beef in the center of the table, along with a few side dishes. Amy and Sharon temporarily put aside their questioning as they all served themselves from the platter.

Jenny took enough food to keep her plate from looking bare, but she didn't have much of an appetite. That might have had something to do with the constant, unnerving pressure of Ken's thigh against hers. Or it could be because of those melting looks he kept sending her way. The last thing she was worried about at the moment was food. She wasn't sure how much more of this she could take and still manage to remember that it didn't mean anything. If he kept this up, he might not be safe from her in the car on the way home.

"How am I doing?" Ken's voice in her ear startled her.

"What?"

"How's the performance? Am I a good enough boyfriend to convince them?"

"I think you're doing too well. I'll never convince them that we've broken up after the way you've been all over me like this."

"I guess that means you'll get to dump me."

"And then they'll have me committed, after they've dragged me to you and forced me to recant."

"So, should I do something slightly obnoxious?"

She shook her head. "No, then they'd really think we were both crazy. You can't change character halfway through. But it wouldn't hurt you to tone it down a bit. We want them to think we're at least waiting until we get home and not jumping in the back seat as soon as we're back in the parking lot."

"You could say you broke up with me because I'm a sex maniac."

"Oh, look at you two," Amy said before Jenny could kick him under the table for that remark. Jenny felt her face become warm. How ironic that Amy had taken a conversation about toning down their romantic antics for a lovebird snugglefest. Her friends weren't going to be able to forget this, even if she and Ken managed to stage a spectacular fight on the way out of the restaurant.

Ken didn't help matters when he reached with his napkin to dab at her chin. "There, now it's all gone," he said. "You had a bit of sauce on your lip."

She licked her lip, but didn't taste any sauce there. She hadn't eaten enough tonight to have managed to get sauce on her face. Maintaining her smile while she gave Ken a light kick in the ankle under the table, she said, "This is fun. It's been too long since we all got together like this."

The group settled into a more normal conversation and Jenny relaxed. Ken was behaving better, aside from the sauce incident. He even managed to bring Jack and Craig out of their shells to join the conversation, rather than letting the women run away with it. That was a relief for Jenny. The men weren't likely to probe for personal information.

When they finished eating, Sharon rose and picked up

her purse. "I think I'm going to dash into the ladies' room. Anyone else?"

Jenny said, "I'll come with you," before Ken could make any remarks. Not that he'd even started to say anything, but the way he was acting tonight, she wouldn't put it past him. For a moment, she thought he was going to make her crawl across his lap to get out of the booth, but after a second's hesitation, he slid out of the booth and helped her up.

Amy joined them, and as soon as the trio entered the ladies' room, both Amy and Sharon turned on Jenny. "It looks to me like someone really likes you," Amy trilled.

"What was all that about being just friends?" Sharon added.

"Well, we were, until tonight," Jenny hedged. "I don't know what got into him."

"Girl, it looks like this could be your lucky night. I just hope you're prepared," Amy said. "Let's see, I think I might have something in here." She dug around in her purse, but Jenny stopped her.

"Amy!" she exclaimed, glancing around to make sure no one else was listening. "It's not like that. And I don't need anything. Really."

Amy and Sharon exchanged a glance, then shrugged. "You're right. I bet he's a real gentleman," Sharon said. "But if I were you, I'd start thinking of what I like in jewelry." She wiggled the fingers of her left hand to make her point.

"I barely know the guy," Jenny protested. "We've only gone out a few times."

"But he definitely has some interest in you," Amy said. "Trust me."

"You really think so?" Jenny unsuccessfully fought back the flicker of hope. If her friends were so convinced, maybe there was something there. The thought made her legs go watery. That was the last thing she needed right now. Not only was Ken bad news, he admitted he was bad news.

"Yes, I really think so," Sharon assured her. "The way he looks at you almost makes me swoon. Heck, if Jack weren't here, and if you weren't my friend, I'd be after that man. I think you've found yourself a keeper."

The three women touched up their lipstick and powdered their noses. Jenny studied her reflection in the mirror. She looked disgustingly like the girl next door, not an object of desire, not the kind of woman a man would look at in such a way that it affected other women. But as Amy had said, she had kissed a lot of frogs. Maybe it was her time.

"Where should we go next?" she asked the others.

"We could go dancing. I'm sure there's someone decent playing at Billy Bob's." Sharon winked at Jenny. "And there's all sorts of nice, dark corners there."

That was the last thing Jenny needed. She'd done more than enough dancing with Ken, and she knew the effect it had on her. She didn't think country music would dilute that effect at all. The way her hormones were acting tonight, she'd only end up doing something stupid and ultimately get herself hurt. Again.

"Why don't we just look around?" Jenny suggested. "This is a great place for people-watching, and they have that little carnival midway just outside the depot."

"Good idea," Amy said. "Then if we stumble on something fun to do, we can do that."

Back in the restaurant, the men were settling the bill as the women returned. On the way out of the restaurant, Sharon stopped in front of an old-fashioned "Love Tester" machine. It had light bulbs set in it, labeled from

Clammy to Red Hot. Sharon took a quarter from her purse and handed it to Jenny. "Okay, let's see how you rate," she said.

Jenny reluctantly took the quarter and put it into the machine, then clasped the lever. The light bulbs lit up in sequence, running rapidly up and down the scale, finally coming to a stop at the bulb labeled Burning.

"Now it's your turn," Sharon said, handing Ken a quarter. "Let's see if you two are compatible."

He caught Jenny's eye and winked as he inserted the quarter into the slot and clasped the lever. Again, the lights ran up and down the scale, but for him, the Red Hot light lit up, accompanied by a series of bells and whistles.

"Told you so," Sharon whispered into Jenny's ear.

Before Jenny could think of a snappy comeback, Ken slipped his arm around her waist. "So, you're only burning for me, when I'm red hot for you," he said with a teasing grin.

"Maybe you need to do something about that," she said. "Are you worthy of red hot?"

"I guess I'll just have to work on it."

They left the restaurant and wandered through the old railroad depot, which had been converted into little shops and restaurants. An old steam train, beautifully restored, sat on the railroad tracks that ran down the middle of the depot.

When they passed the train, Jenny could see the lights of a small amusement park on the other side of the station. "I think that's an antique carousel they have here," she said.

"Why don't we check it out?" Ken suggested, then called over his shoulder to the others, "We'll meet you back here." Before the others could respond, he'd hustled Jenny toward the midway.

"My lady, your steed awaits," Ken said with a sweeping bow. She took his elbow and let him lead her to the carousel. He bought tickets for the ride, then they stepped onto the platform. "Pick your horse," he said. She chose a white one trimmed in gold. He helped her mount, and even though she was perfectly capable of doing so on her own, she appreciated the gesture.

He then climbed into the saddle of a black charger next to her. "Race you!" he said as the carousel began to move. She laughed and made a show out of kicking her horse into a gallop.

She liked this playful side of him. It came out every so often in a teasing remark. But that night in the hotel bar, she never would have dreamed that she'd see him pretending to race a carousel horse. If she wasn't careful, she could fall hard for Ken, stand-by date or not. She wondered if that was cheating. After all, she'd been the one to lay down the ground rules, and she wouldn't be a good stand-by date if she took it as anything more romantic, no matter how good he was at playing the dashing suitor.

But it was hard to control her feelings. If they were going to continue this stand-by date business, he couldn't go around touching her like he had tonight, or stealing little chances to kiss her. That was never in the stand-by plan. In fact, Jenny couldn't really think of an instance in which a true stand-by date would ever be required to pretend to be a lover.

If they were already breaking the rules, would it hurt to break one more?

The carousel came to a stop, and Ken helped her down from the horse and the platform. As they walked across the Stockyards, looking for the others in the street of recreated Old West saloons, he kept his hand on the back of her waist. They walked up and down the street, looking at the sights and occasionally commenting, but mostly silent. Jenny decided she liked Ken better like this, when he was just being himself rather than pretending to be what he thought she needed. He could be fun and silly, or he could be quiet without feeling the need to fill conversational spaces. His easy silence was more dangerous to her than all his touches and kisses.

About an hour later, the group gathered back in front of the midway. Craig fought to stifle a yawn, then said, "It's been fun, but it's also been a long day. Would anyone mind if we call it a night?"

Jenny looked at her watch and realized how late it was—nearly midnight. Suddenly her own long day caught up with her. "I have to admit, I'm beginning to wilt a bit," she said. The others agreed, and they began to walk back to the parking area as a group. The others peeled off to their cars, and finally Ken and Jenny were left alone.

Ken kept his arm around her as they walked the final stretch to the car. Jenny tried to savor the moment—the starry night sky, the sounds of fun and scent of food wafting from the Stockyards, the feel of Ken's warmth next to her. She could get used to this.

They reached the car, and Ken opened the door for her. She got in and reached over to unlock his door while he was walking around the car. When he got in and started the engine, she said, "That wasn't so bad. It was actually a lot of fun."

"Of course it was fun. And your friends will have plenty to talk about."

"Thanks to you. They'll be calling me tomorrow to find out what happened once we were alone."

"You can tell them we waited until we got home. The back seat was too small."

"That's not what I'm going to tell them. I don't want to give them too many ideas."

"I thought that was the point of all this."

"The point of all this was that having you around meant I got to spend time with my friends even though they're part of couples. I didn't need to convince them that I'm in a hot, passionate affair."

"And why not? I bet they think you could use a hot, passionate affair."

"But what happens later when they ask about you and you're not there anymore? What do I tell them then?"

"All those frogs you've kissed—did they seem like nice guys at first?"

"Of course, or I wouldn't have kissed them in the first place."

"So, tell them I turned out to be yet another frog. I don't know why you're worrying so much about this. I'll be glad to play my part when you need me, until either you or I actually find a real date. I doubt it's going to happen anytime soon for me, and if it happens for you, then you won't have to worry about what your friends think about me."

"You're right," she admitted, but his words didn't offer her a lot of comfort. Maybe she was just being pessimistic, but she had a feeling this whole thing was going to come crashing down on her before long.

Ken left her at her door with a quick hug, not even a kiss on the cheek. As she headed off to her bedroom, Jenny had to chuckle over the difference between what her friends were probably imagining she was doing and what she was really doing. She doubted they'd believe she was going to bed alone, without so much as a kiss good-night.

And for the first time in ages, she wished she had someone else there when she turned out the light.

8

8

Ken popped yet another cheese puff into his mouth and wondered how soon he could leave without it looking too bad. He should have known better than to go to a cocktail party on his own, but he'd hated to subject Jenny to this kind of thing. He needed to be strong, to stand on his own for a change.

Before he could leave, he knew he had to do some mingling with the partners. He wiped his hands on a cocktail napkin, squared his shoulders and marched to where one of the partners stood near his wife, chatting with another couple. Ken didn't want to burst into their conversation, so he lingered on the edge of the group until one of them noticed him. The spouses were introduced to him, and he felt their inquiring eyes when he didn't introduce anyone. He fumbled through some small talk, but as the conversation seemed to center on something that had happened at the company Christmas party, he quickly made his escape.

He'd never noticed how awkward these things could be. Before, he'd always had someone with him, so even if he was shut out of a conversation, he had someone to talk to. Introducing the date also gave him a way to start a conversation or worm his way into one that was already taking place.

Glancing around the room, he searched for his usual office buddies. They were all in a group in a corner. He wandered over and stood nearby, waiting for a lull in the conversation so he could join in. He might as well have been invisible. Not in the mood for answering questions about where his date was, he moved away. In this crowd, he doubted the partners would even know who was there, so he decided it wouldn't fatally damage his career if he left.

A hand on his shoulder as he headed toward the door froze him, and his blood ran cold when he turned to find himself looking one of the senior partners in his group in the eye. *Oh, great,* he thought, *caught the one time I try to sneak out.* "Good evening, Randolph," he said.

"I just wanted to catch you before you left. My wife and I are having a few people from the firm over for dinner this weekend. I was wondering if you could join us. It's Saturday night, and I hope your lady friend will be able to make it, too."

Ken started to ask what lady friend, then caught himself. He was one of three unmarried men in his group, and the other two had steady girlfriends. The last time he'd been invited to dinner by Randolph, he'd still been with Kristen. An invitation from the boss was considered an honor. He couldn't turn this down. "We'll be there," he said. "I'll look forward to it.

"Good. I'll make sure you get an invitation."

As he completed his escape, Ken hoped Jenny would be free. If anything fit the definition of an occasion requiring an emergency stand-by date, this was it.

It had been a macaroni-and-cheese kind of day. Jenny usually tried to eat well, even if most of it was takeout, but there were those days when nothing but comfort food would do. The worst days were the ones when she came home wanting nothing more than macaroni and cheese—the kind made from a box with the powdered cheese sauce mix.

She took a bite of macaroni, straight from the saucepan, and felt herself relax as she lost herself in the pages of the book she was reading. This was one of those times when she was grateful to be single. She didn't think a married woman could get away with eating macaroni and cheese straight out of the pot while she read at the table.

The phone rang before she could polish off the whole pot. She shoved the pan into the refrigerator before answering the phone so she wouldn't be tempted to eat any more. "Hello?" she said, picking up the phone just before the answering machine came on.

"Hi, it's Ken."

"Hi," she said, wishing she could think of something a little more clever. "What's up?"

"Do you have plans for this weekend?"

"None that I can think of," she said. "Why?"

"One of the partners in my firm is having a few of us over for dinner. It's kind of a couples dinner party, so they're expecting me to bring someone. Last time I was invited over, Kristen was there."

She cringed. Not only was this another stand-by date, but it was a difficult one. A dinner party with someone else's boss wasn't her idea of a good time, but she also couldn't in good conscience leave Ken alone to face the evening. "When is it?" she asked.

"Next Saturday at seven."

She didn't have to look at her calendar to know she was free. Her alternative was staying home and watching old movies on cable or reading. As pleasant as that sounded to her, she wouldn't mind the opportunity to get out of the house. "I could make that," she said. "What's the dress code?"

"The invitation said 'informal.' I'll probably wear a jacket and tie."

"Okay, I can handle that. What angle are you looking for here? Someone to impress your boss with grace and class, or a knockout to make your co-workers jealous?"

He laughed. "You are a pro at this sort of thing, aren't you? What about something in the middle? Classy enough to impress the boss, sexy enough to impress my co-workers."

She smiled as she thought about trying to carry off that kind of act. "We'll see what I can come up with," she said with a sultry purr.

"I can hardly wait." His voice was soft and husky, and it sent shivers up her spine. "I'll pick you up at six-thirty on Saturday."

"I'll see you then."

Jenny hung up the phone and took a deep breath. Ken had an interesting effect on her. He made her feel like a giggling schoolgirl and a sexy temptress all at the same time. She wondered what he'd do to her if they were actually involved romantically. She'd probably lose herself entirely and dissolve into a puddle of goo whenever he touched her. As nice as that might feel from time to time, the thought of being constantly in that state was somewhat terrifying.

But they weren't romantically involved, so she could have a little fun with this, knowing it wouldn't go anywhere, and she had the perfect dress for the occasion. She couldn't wait to see how he reacted.

When Jenny opened the door Saturday night, Ken's first inclination was to skip the dinner party and stay at

Jenny's place all evening. She looked terrific, and he wanted her all to himself. She wore a simple dress that managed to be elegant and sexy at the same time. It didn't expose much skin and it wasn't form-fitting, but when she moved, it hinted at the body underneath. She wore her hair up, with just a few tendrils framing her face. He hadn't ever seen her this way.

On second thought, they really should go out, he decided. It would be a shame for her to have wasted all that effort for nothing, and he wanted to show her off.

"You look great," he said, trying not to gape at her.

Her cheeks turned a shade pinker. "Will I do?" she asked, doing a little turn so he could see the full effect.

"You'll do," he said. She'd more than do. She was a knockout. Why hadn't he noticed that from the beginning? Come to think of it, he had noticed, but he'd been trying to ignore it. The way she looked now, it was awfully hard to avoid. He needed to get her away from here while he still had the willpower. He was dangerously close to slipping into his old ways. "Are you ready to go?" he forced himself to ask, even though he wasn't ready.

"I'm as ready as I'll ever be."

"Good. Let's go."

As Ken drove to Randolph's home, he couldn't keep himself from stealing glances at Jenny. Before tonight, he had thought of her as pretty. Now, she generated a totally different reaction in him. She appeared oblivious to his scrutiny.

"Is there anything I should know before we get there?" she asked.

"Like what?" he replied, startled out of his thoughts.

"Well, anyone I should watch out for, anyone I should particularly try to impress, that sort of thing."

Ken hadn't been thinking of work, so he had to readjust his train of thought. "Just impress the boss. I don't really have any enemies, so there's no one to watch out for."

"You don't have any enemies that you know of," she corrected with a sly smile. "Need any spying done?"

He shook his head. "Don't worry about it." He could imagine that she could do quite a good job of spying, with her innocent face, but he didn't want her away from him long enough to have a chance to learn anything.

The Jenny who came with him to the dinner party was very much like the Jenny he'd first met that night in the hotel lounge. She was bright, witty, articulate and just a bit seductive, without making any effort to be that way. And he couldn't get over how gorgeous she was.

It was sheer torture being next to her the whole evening, watching her but not daring to touch her. He wondered if she knew the effect she was having on every man in the room, and most especially on him. But she seemed so entirely unselfconscious about her power that it served only to increase the effect.

What would she do if he kissed her? Ken wondered. Not in public when they were carrying out their act, but alone, when there was no one else to see? He knew what it felt like to kiss her, but he wondered what it might be like if it meant something.

There wasn't much use in thinking about it, he reminded himself. She was the one who had set the terms for their relationship, and he'd accepted them the first time he'd asked her out. If only he'd simply invited her to the picnic rather than saying he needed an emergency stand-by date. But at the time, he hadn't known how much he would come to like her. It was probably for the best, though. He wouldn't be good for her. She'd been hurt before, and he didn't want to be the next one to cause her pain. He wasn't sure he was capable of the kind of relationship she needed and deserved.

He jumped when she touched his arm lightly to get his attention. "Are you ready for dessert?" she asked.

"Oh, yes, sure," he stammered. *Real smooth,* he scolded himself. Here Jenny was, playing the gracious, elegant guest, and he was the one acting like a rube. His arm still tingled where she'd touched him. If just a touch could do that much, he was afraid to let himself get any closer to her.

It was a relief when the party began breaking up, but the relief was quickly replaced with dread. Now he had to be alone with her, and Ken was determined not to allow his imagination to get the better of him. Once more, he reminded himself of the pledge he'd made weeks ago. He wasn't going to rush into anything rash just because he was with a beautiful woman.

It was getting more and more difficult to keep that promise to himself.

Back at Jenny's house at the end of the evening, they paused outside the front door. "That wasn't so bad," she said with a smile. "And I thought lawyers would be dull."

"Hey! Watch what you're saying. Some of the nicest people I know are lawyers." Okay, this was good, Ken thought. He was making conversation, and sounding reasonably intelligent.

She raised an eyebrow. "Whatever you say." Opening the front door, she turned back to him and said, "Do you want to come in?"

He wasn't exactly sure how she meant the invitation,

but he wouldn't have turned it down for the world, even though he was sure it wasn't a good idea. He followed her into the front hallway, where she turned to face him.

"Would you like a root beer float?" she asked.

That wasn't exactly what he had in mind, but it sounded good, and it was all she had offered. "Sure," he said and followed her into the kitchen.

She went to work preparing the floats as he cast about for something to say.

"I'm really starting to see your point about the trouble of singles mixing with couples," he said at last, leaning on the kitchen counter near where she was working. "I made the mistake of going to an office party alone last week, and it was miserable. I felt like I didn't exist. Then there's Greg. He used to be my best friend, and now I can't think of much to say to him."

"That's because you still have the Kristen issue between you," she said, spooning ice cream into glasses. "If he'd married anyone else, you just would have had to get used to him with his wife. But since you have a history with Kristen, you not only have to get used to his new status, you have to get used to her new position in your life. That's not easy."

"I'm surprised at you."

"Why's that?" she asked, pausing in her work to look up at him.

"You're defending the married. I thought you were ready to leap on any injustice perpetrated on single people."

She put the ice cream back in the freezer and took a bottle of root beer from the refrigerator. "I don't have anything against married people. I just don't like the way the world treats single people. Married people can't help it if they have different things to talk about. I only mind it when they're so excited about being married that they try to get all their single friends married off." She slammed the root beer bottle onto the counter for emphasis, then handed him a glass.

He took a sip of root beer, then asked, "So, you don't have anything against being part of a couple?"

"Not as long as it's on my terms rather than because someone else can't bear for me to be single." She carried her glass to the kitchen table and sat down.

He followed her and sat across the table from her. "You know, it's funny," he said, twirling his straw around in his float.

"What's funny? Two grown adults drinking root beer floats on a Saturday night? I do this all the time."

"It's funny how I never thought about what it was like to be single until I met you."

She raised an eyebrow. "I think I'll take that as a compliment."

"What I mean is, I was so busy being worried about not being in a couple that I forgot about being me. And you and I both noticed how our lives changed once others started seeing us as a couple."

"Boy, did it change. I haven't been out this many weeks in a row in ages. I think I've had more dates in the past month than I had in the whole year before. Well, sort of dates. At least I was out of my house in the company of a man."

Sort of dates? He winced and ate the ice cream out of his glass. Was that supposed to mean she didn't consider him a real date? "What's this 'sort of' business?" he asked, trying to grin in spite of himself.

"No offense, but lunch with your parents or dinner with your boss isn't really my idea of a date—even if it's more of a social life than I've had in ages." She licked a bit of ice cream off her lower lip, and his own tongue quivered in response. This woman was getting under his skin.

"So, how do you define a real date?" Ken asked, leaning closer to her.

Jenny frowned in thought for a moment, then said with a chuckle, "It's been so long, I think I've forgotten."

"But if you could create your perfect date, what would it be?"

Her eyes took on a faraway look. "I don't think it matters so much what you do. Who you're with is more important. I think it could be an incredibly romantic evening just ordering pizza and talking all night if you're with the right person. And the Vienna Opera Ball could be a real drag with the wrong person."

"You're still not answering my question. What is Jenny Forrest's idea of the perfect date with the right person?"

"With the right person? Do you mean the fabled Mr. Right, once known as Prince Charming, the guy I've been kissing all these frogs to find?"

"None other."

"Then it wouldn't matter what we did, once we got away from the lily pad. I suppose it would be nice to have dinner in a really good restaurant, with candlelight, attentive service and soft music. Afterward, maybe a moonlight stroll or a carriage ride. Then we'd talk all night and watch the sun come up."

"Talk all night? Wouldn't you run out of things to say?"

"Not if we're getting to know each other, sharing with each other, the way..." Her voice trailed off, but he had a feeling he knew what she meant. The way they had talked the night they met. They very easily could have talked until dawn.

"But just talking? That's all you'd do all night?"

She blushed. "I'm assuming this is fairly early in the relationship, and I'm not that kind of girl."

"That just shows where your mind is," he said with a chuckle. "I was thinking more in terms of dancing. And maybe a kiss or two."

"Just one or two?"

"Well, once you get started, you tend to lose count. One kiss leads to the next, and the next, and after that, they sort of blur together so it's hard to tell where one ends and the next begins."

Jenny had leaned forward, too, her hands clasped around her glass. Her eyes were wide and dark, the pupils crowding out the green, and her lips were parted, moist and tempting. All he had to do was lean forward just a bit more....

Then he stopped himself. He'd started talking the way he had just to get a reaction out of her, but he'd affected himself, too. Maybe he'd better get out of there now, before he did something he'd regret later when he was a little more sane. "Speaking of talking until dawn, if we're not careful, we'll manage that tonight. I think I'd better be going."

"You're probably right," she said with a nod and a deep breath as she stood.

"Thanks for the ice cream," Ken said when they reached the front door. "You managed to salvage the evening." He started to step outside, then turned back. "I'll see you later?" he said, turning the statement into a question.

"You owe me one now, so you can bet you'll see me later." She said it with a wry smile that made her lips look like they really needed to be kissed. He shook her hand, then as he continued to clasp it, he bent forward and gave her a gentle kiss on the lips. He backed away quickly, before he let his earlier speech about all-night kisses get the better of either of them.

Back in his car, Ken loosened his tie, then gripped the steering wheel until his knuckles whitened. It was a test, that's what it was. He was being tested to see if he could keep his promise not to fall head over heels for the first woman he saw, just because he was lonely. This time, he was going to think with his head instead of his heart—or anything else.

Even more important than the promise he'd made himself was the unspoken promise to Jenny. He couldn't bear the thought of joining her parade of frogs and he didn't want to do anything to hurt her. Right now, he was bad news for any woman, and most especially Jenny.

That was it? Jenny stared at the closed front door as she kicked off her high-heeled dress shoes and rubbed her feet. She had dressed to kill and he had looked at her all night like he wished he were alone with her, then he'd given her the most compelling discourse on kissing she'd ever heard, only to leave her with a quick peck at the door—a kiss he could have given his sister. What had she done wrong? She thought she'd struck a nice balance, sexy enough to keep his attention, but demure enough not to embarrass him in front of his boss. Then they'd had that bizarre and wonderful conversation over root beer floats in her kitchen. She hadn't wanted to say it at the time, but that part of the evening could easily have fit into her definition of a great date.

You're doing it again, Jen, she thought, padding in

her stocking feet to the kitchen. Every time a man looked at her twice, she started getting all mushy over him. And every time, he wasn't nearly as mushy over her. She'd outgrown that kind of schoolgirl crush. Now she was a grown woman with a nice male friend. She didn't need to start dreaming about him.

She'd let herself grow dependent on him, she decided as she set about cleaning up the kitchen. Before she'd met him, a Saturday night alone hadn't bothered her a bit. Now she spent the week wondering what they'd do the next weekend. Before things got out of hand, she would have to wean herself from him. Then she remembered one more event that was coming up. She'd been planning to ask him tonight, but he'd distracted her with all that talk of real dates and kisses.

Okay, so she'd wean herself after this weekend.

Ken got home late the next Monday night. He had spent most of the workday listening to his co-workers' comments about Jenny. He hadn't been the only one she'd affected that night. Even his boss had been impressed. Ken wondered what they'd think if they knew he and Jenny had shared no more than ice cream together, and that he'd left her at the door with a quick kiss.

His workload didn't make allowances for water-cooler chat, so he had to stay late at the office to finish after all the interruptions during the day. He got home to find the message-waiting indicator on his answering machine blinking. "I forgot to call Mom," he groaned. More than likely, that's what the message was. He hit the play button and waited for a gentle lecture and a bit of prodding about how things were progressing with Jenny. He really did need to come up with a breakup excuse before that situation got out of control, he thought.

Instead he got a husky female voice with a soft Texas drawl. Jenny. "Hi, Ken, it's Jenny," the voice on the tape said. "It's time for you to repay the favor. I need an escort for an event one of my clients is putting on next weekend. The good news is that this isn't really work-related. They just need warm bodies to fill seats. The bad news is it's black tie. I hope you have a tux handy. It's Saturday night. Give me a call and let me know if you can make it."

He grinned. Black tie? He wondered what she'd be wearing. It couldn't be much more impressive than that black dress she'd worn Saturday night, but it was bound to show off a little more skin. Then he blinked and shook his head to clear it. What was he thinking? She had invited him as a safe date. Behaving like a drooling fool wasn't what she'd consider safe.

He dropped his briefcase on the kitchen counter and dialed Jenny's number. "Hi, it's me. I got your message," he said when she answered.

"Can you make it?" she asked without preamble.

"I'll be there with bells on."

"I'd prefer it if you wore a tux."

"That, too. Is a powder-blue one with a ruffled shirt okay? I got it for my high-school prom and I almost never get a chance to wear it anymore."

She laughed. "I'm sure you'll stand out in the crowd. But I hope we don't clash. I was planning to wear blue, too."

"You think I'm joking, don't you?" he said, teasing her. He settled onto a bar stool and pulled off his tie. He liked talking to her like this, without the external tensions that seemed to surround all their dates. He wouldn't mind prolonging this conversation.

"If you aren't joking, you'll really owe me one. I'll have to make you go to a costume party with me, dressed as the rear part of a horse."

"I've played that role a few times in my life. Once I even wore the costume to go with it."

"I'm sure you have." If he wasn't mistaken, there was a flirtatious tone in her voice.

"So, you're going to be wearing blue," he said. "The dress from your reunion?"

"Same color. Different dress. You'll just have to wait to see it."

"Is it anything like that dress you wore Saturday?"

"You liked that one?" He detected a hint of curiosity in her voice.

"Very much. And so did everyone else. I've been hearing about it all day at work."

There was a pause on the other end of the line, then she said, "It's nothing like that dress. Just wait." On the last two words, she let her voice drop to a throaty whisper. If he'd been in the same room with her, he wouldn't have been able to resist kissing her down the side of her neck to the hollow at the base of her throat.

"I've got it marked on my calendar," Ken said, his own voice husky with desire. Right now, he could shoot himself for having walked away from her Saturday night. He could have given her at least one chance to clarify the rules for an emergency stand-by date. "What time do we need to be there?"

"The event's at eight at the university. It's a benefit concert sponsored by my client, followed by a champagne reception. We could almost walk from my house. That would probably be easier than trying to park."

"Okay, what do you say I get there at seven? And I'll wear my comfortable dress shoes."

"I didn't know such things existed. I'm planning to stock up on blister treatments."

"I'll see you then. I'll be the one in a blue tuxedo."

"And you'll die very soon thereafter." She said it with a low chuckle. He hung up the phone, half tempted to make a visit to the Goodwill store so he could carry through on his threat, but he wouldn't do that to her for a work-related event. The tuxedo hanging in his closet was the classic style, black with a waistcoat.

And he couldn't wait to see that dress.

9

She was certainly going to send this stand-by date relationship out with a bang, Jenny thought as she did a twirl around her bedroom in time with the music coming from her radio. The dress was everything she had promised him, and she'd been saving it for a special occasion. It was a dark blue silk, with narrow shoulder straps, a plunging back and a neckline low enough to show a hint of cleavage—even with her slender build. Tailored so that it followed every curve of her body, it left little to the imagination. A slit up the thigh revealed plenty of leg. She had left her hair loose around her shoulders, and she wore just a hint of shimmery makeup.

She did a seductive move she never would have dared on a real dance floor in front of people, then posed in front of her mirror. She was a knockout, if she said so herself.

The doorbell rang, and Jenny slipped her feet into low-heeled evening shoes on her way to the door. She'd danced for hours in these shoes, so she hoped they'd work for walking.

Ken's reaction when she opened the door was everything she'd hoped for. His eyes widened, his mouth opened, and it took him a few seconds to say anything. Contrary to his threat, he was dressed in a classic black tuxedo, and if ever a man was born to wear a tux, it was Ken. She'd forgotten how gorgeous he'd been the night she met him.

"You look great," they said in unison, then laughed.

"I see you decided to update your tuxedo," she said with a grin. "I'm glad. I don't think powder blue is your color."

"But blue is certainly your color," he said, looking her up and down. Although he didn't touch her physically, the touch of his eyes was almost tangible. She felt her skin grow warm under his gaze. Right now, she wished they'd never tried to define this relationship as "safe," and from the way he was looking at her, he was wishing the same thing. Would it hurt to break the rules just once? They didn't have to become deeply involved emotionally or for long enough to cause pain, but tonight she really wished he'd touch her the way he was looking at her.

"Are you up to walking?" she asked, having to cough to clear the catch in her throat. "It's just a few blocks, and the parking situation will be difficult."

"It's a lovely evening for a walk," he said, bowing and extending his elbow to her. She locked the door, then laughed as she took his arm, and they strolled down the sidewalk. It *was* a lovely evening for a walk, a warm Texas summer night. She was perfectly comfortable in her bare dress, but she imagined he was a bit warm in that tuxedo.

"Now it's your turn to brief me," he said as they walked. "Is there anything I should be aware of?"

"Just be nice to my client and behave like a gentleman. This is a benefit concert my client is sponsoring. It didn't sell out, but to keep there from being empty seats, my client invited a few people, including me, to come. I don't normally get to do things this glamorous with my job."

"What kind of concert is this?" He grinned roguishly, then added, "I hope it won't put me to sleep."

"It's mostly classical, with a guest artist. But they may throw in one or two pop numbers. And don't worry, if you nod off, I'll kick you awake."

"I really don't think it will be a problem."

"It better not be," she said with a warning glare. But she couldn't maintain the glare for long. She felt too good. Giving his arm a little squeeze, she had to contain her sigh of joy. She'd been wanting an evening like this for ages—a classy event, a gorgeous guy and all sorts of possibilities. This was something else that might fit her definition of a perfect real date.

The lobby of the university auditorium was packed with people in evening finery. Jenny spotted her client, but he was surrounded by people, so she didn't think this would be a good time for introductions. She'd catch him at the reception afterward. She and Ken had arrived just as the doors to the concert hall opened, so they entered and took their seats.

Jenny didn't think Ken would have much trouble staying awake during the concert. The music was passionate and stirring, but it wasn't the music that kept her alert. It was the sensation of Ken next to her. She could feel the wool of his tuxedo sleeve against her bare arm, and when he leaned over to whisper a comment to her, his warm breath tickled the back of her neck. Every so often, she caught him looking at her. She hoped that was a good sign. The way she'd dressed tonight, she should be able to grab the attention of any man. If not, she might as well give up now.

The concert ended with a standing ovation, then the

audience flowed into the lobby. While the concert was taking place, the caterers had moved in, transforming the lobby into a culinary extravaganza. Champagne flowed and waiters circulated with trays of fancy canapés.

Ken took two glasses of champagne from the tray of a passing waiter and handed one to Jenny. Then he raised his glass to her. "To emergency stand-by dates, may they always be there when we need them."

She tried not to cringe at his use of her own term. She had invited him this evening more because she wanted his company than because she needed an escort, even if she was planning to break herself of the habit after tonight. Raising her own glass, she said, "And may we develop lives so we don't need emergency stand-by dates very often."

"I'll drink to that," he said, clinking his glass against hers. She took a sip of champagne and let the bubbles tickle her tongue.

After taking a swallow of his drink, Ken said, "I think I'm getting pretty good at this escort thing. I hear you can make good money in this business."

Refusing to rise to his bait, she said, "I'll give you a good reference if you need one."

He laughed and put his arm around her waist. "But you haven't seen a full demonstration of all my skills."

She took another sip of her drink as she regarded him. "I know you can dance. You're good at fetching drinks. What more is there?"

"Just point me in the direction of your client and see how well I impress business associates."

She'd rather hoped he was planning to demonstrate a different kind of skill, but preferably not in public. They handed their empty glasses off to a waiter, then she led him over to where her client was holding court.

"Mr. Richards!" she said to get his attention.

He turned to her, held out his hands and said, "My dear Jennifer," then kissed her on the cheek. "I'm so glad you could come tonight."

"It's been a wonderful event," she said, then pulled Ken forward. "I'd like you to meet Ken Parks. Ken, this is Ron Richards, of Richards Enterprises."

Ken shook hands and said a few words about how impressive the event was. They made small talk for a few minutes, then Jenny excused herself and Ken, so Richards could return to his associates.

"See, didn't I handle that well?" Ken asked as he took another couple of glasses of champagne.

She cocked her head to one side and gave him a mock appraising frown. "I'm afraid I might need a demonstration of some of your other skills before I could give you a full reference."

"They're playing the wrong music, and there isn't much of a dance floor, so I'm afraid I can't show you how brilliant I am with a tango. For now, you'll have to see how good I am at foraging for food at a cocktail party."

She wasn't really hungry, although she knew she shouldn't be drinking this much champagne on an empty stomach. Her head was starting to feel as full of bubbles as the champagne. The funny feeling owed more to the atmosphere of the evening than to the champagne itself, but she was glad she hadn't driven here.

After sampling the canapés and drinking at least one more glass of champagne—she was starting to lose count—Ken bent to whisper in her ear, "Do you want to stay much longer?"

Actually, she had been dying to leave for a full twenty minutes. She wanted him to herself, and she wanted to find out if all her preparations for the evening had been in vain. What she told him was, "I'm ready to leave if you are."

"Let's go," he said, taking her arm and nearly pulling her off her feet. She wondered if he was as anxious to get to her place as she was, and if it was for the same reasons.

The few blocks from the university to Jenny's house seemed like miles to Ken. Part of it was the tuxedo jacket that wasn't designed for walking in July in Texas. And part of it was Jenny in that dress. If it had been up to him, they never would have gone anywhere that evening. Even better, tonight she hadn't been acting like a stand-by date. She had touched him and allowed him to touch her, even though no one who mattered was watching.

She hadn't oversold the dress. It was stunning. But what was most stunning about it was the way it revealed and hinted at her form. It was bare enough to show plenty of creamy white skin, but even where it covered her, the silky fabric clung to her body, leaving nothing to the imagination. His fingers itched to touch her, and to touch far more than the arms and waist he'd been limited to so far this evening.

He stumbled going up her doorstep, and she laughed. "I think you'd better come in and have some coffee before you try driving home," she said.

His stumble had more to do with watching her than the amount of champagne he'd had, but he didn't argue with her. He followed her inside. "The living room's in there. You go ahead and get comfortable while I make the coffee."

He followed her directions and found himself in a

cozy little room. A big fireplace dominated one side of the room. An overstuffed sofa and chairs were arranged on the glossy wood floor, facing an entertainment center with a television and stereo system. There were a few compact disc cases lying on top of the stereo, and he picked them up. Mostly classical music, he noted. Some jazz. Funny, they'd never discussed musical tastes. That was one more thing he didn't know about her.

Hearing footsteps in the hallway, he turned around just in time to see Jenny enter the room. "The coffee should be ready in a minute or two," she said. He stared at her, transfixed. The lamplight shimmered on the fabric of her dress and gave her skin a soft glow. Simultaneously, they took a step toward each other. She paused, and he moved the rest of the way, until he was standing at less than an arm's reach from her, so close, but still with a gulf between them, one they'd yet to cross. They'd touched before, even kissed, but always as part of some kind of act put on to impress someone else. But now it was just the two of them, no make-believe couple, no need to put on a show. Just Ken and Jenny, and Ken wanted Jenny more than he'd ever wanted anything else.

"You look wonderful tonight," he said. His voice came out sounding rough. "You really weren't lying about that dress." She responded with a bashful smile. Taking that as a sign of encouragement, he decided to cross the gulf between safe date and something else entirely. He reached forward to brush her hair off her shoulder, then traced her collarbone with one finger, until he got to the dress's slender strap, which he pushed off her shoulder. Then he ran his fingers back across her shoulder to the hollow of her throat and down to the plunging neckline of the dress.

She shivered, breathing heavily, but she made no

move to step away from him or otherwise stop him. He ran his finger slowly up her neck to trace her jawline, then stroke her cheek. Savoring the velvety softness of her skin, he turned his hand to stroke her cheek again with the backs of his fingers. She sighed and closed her eyes, but otherwise did nothing. He was close enough to smell her perfume, a warm fragrance with hints of vanilla and musk. It suited her.

Then he could hold himself back no longer. He bent and kissed her, no brotherly peck this time, but an all-out possession of her mouth. Her lips were as soft as her skin had been beneath his fingers, and they yielded willingly to his kiss.

After a second's hesitation, Jenny put her arms around him and laced her fingers at the nape of his neck, pulling him closer to her. She met every touch of his tongue with one of her own as he gathered her body into his arms and drew her up against him. He ran his fingers lightly up and down her back, still savoring the sensation of her skin against his fingertips.

"Ken," she whispered after a full minute of kissing.

"Mmm-hmmm," he murmured, trailing kisses down the side of her neck.

She arched her neck to accommodate him, then said a moment later, "Maybe this would be a little easier if we weren't standing up. I'm getting a crick in my neck."

Jenny probably could have found something a little more appropriate to say under the circumstances, but she *was* getting a crick in her neck, and she didn't want to have to stop what they were doing because of severe neck pain.

Ken froze for a second, then he grinned, his eyes crinkling at the corners. "Ever the pragmatist, aren't you,

Jen? Shall we adjourn to the sofa?" His voice was soft, with a light, teasing tone, but his eyes were locked on hers.

He took her hand, guided her to the sofa, then lowered her onto the cushions. "Now, where were we?" he asked. "Somewhere about here, I think." He drew her into the circle of his arm, brushed the hair back from her face, then bent once more to kiss her. She felt like she was melting into his embrace as his warm hands caressed her skin and his lips burned against hers.

Now that the unspoken barrier between them had been broken and she no longer had to pretend to feel nothing more than friendship, she opened herself to the emotions that had been growing all this time within her. Instead of denying them, she embraced them—and embraced him. Tentatively at first, but growing bolder with each move, she touched his cheek, stroked his jaw, grasped his shoulder.

Her touch seemed to inflame him further. His kisses became less gentle, more demanding, and she responded in kind. She lost herself in his kisses, his touches, his embraces, and for once, she didn't fear the feeling. She welcomed this melding of bodies and souls. How could she have denied herself this for so long? A slight doubt lingered in the back of her mind, reminding her she was only setting herself up for another heartbreak, but she banished the thought. She had plenty of time to be sensible later. Now she wanted to enjoy the madness.

Ken placed both his hands on her shoulders and held her firmly while he gave her a deep, exploring kiss, as if he wanted to consume her whole in that moment. Then he pulled away, keeping his hands on her shoulders. She felt an ache at the sudden distance. "I'm sure both of us could keep going on like this indefinitely," he said hoarsely, "but if we don't stop now, we'll both regret it in the morning."

Jenny wanted to argue, to tell him she would regret nothing, even if it was for just one night, but in her heart, she knew he was right. The doubts were already there, as much as she tried to ignore them. She nodded as she bit her lip. "You're probably right," she whispered. "I think the coffee's done by now, if you want any."

He shook his head and ran a hand through his hair. "I'm okay. And I'd like to get some sleep tonight."

She nodded. "Okay."

He shifted positions on the sofa, so that he was sitting next to her rather than embracing her. "I want you to know that this wasn't exactly on my agenda for tonight. I just...I guess I just couldn't stop myself." He gave her a shaky grin. "That sounds pretty lame, doesn't it? I guess I've blown it as a good safe date."

"You didn't notice me stopping you, did you?"

He raised an eyebrow. "Not exactly."

"But you're right, this kind of violates the idea of a stand-by date." She grinned. "You're the lawyer. Maybe we should have had you draw up a contract before we got into this. Then we'd know better what to expect and where we stood."

"I thought you were the expert on stand-by dates."

She sighed and shook her head. "I wouldn't call myself an expert. I just think it's a good idea. I've never had to deal with a stand-by date relationship that lasted more than one or two dates. This whole thing has been different."

"It looks like we'll either have to change the definition, or change what we call ourselves."

"You mean, date for real?"

"We could try. Tonight may have been just one of

those things, or it may have meant something. I'd like to know which."

Jenny forced back her habitual panic. True, Ken didn't have a great track record, but then again, neither did she. It was a risk. But right now, she'd risk anything to be kissed like that again. "Okay. Let's give it a shot."

"What are you doing next Saturday night?"

"No dinner parties, no gathering with friends, no family events. Looks like I could be available, as long as it's just us, going out."

"Okay, what about dinner someplace nice? We can talk, like we did back when we first met. And we won't have to be anything but who we are. No pretending to be anything else, no living up to anyone else's expectations. Just Ken and Jenny. What do you say?"

"I think it sounds wonderful," Jenny said. And terrifying.

"Great. What do you say I pick you up at eight. Feel free to dress up."

"Does that mean you're wearing the powder-blue tuxedo?" she asked, fighting back a grin.

"You can count on it. It was still at the cleaners tonight, but it will be ready by next week."

She rolled her eyes. "I can hardly wait."

"Neither can I." Both of them laughed. It was hard to believe that just a few minutes ago they'd been kissing passionately, on the brink of what could have been some incredibly intense lovemaking. Now they were laughing and teasing each other like old friends. Jenny's doubts returned. Had tonight been just an attack of loneliness and a need for the human contact she had denied herself for so long, or did it mean that something really was building between them? She supposed she'd find out soon enough.

Ken glanced at his watch. "I guess I'd better be going. It's pretty late."

He stood, straightened his jacket and tie, then made his way to the door, with Jenny following. At the door, he turned to face her. "Thank you for inviting me. I enjoyed the concert." He gave her a roguish grin. "And I really enjoyed what happened after the concert."

Ducking her head bashfully, she said, "So did I."

"I'll see you next weekend. And I'll call you sometime before then."

"I guess this is the end of our stand-by date relationship."

"I suppose so."

"No more games, no more pretending to be anything more than we are."

"No, no more games. I don't know that we need to necessarily come clean to our friends and families, but we don't have to impress anyone but each other."

"Good. That should be a relief. It's a miracle no one figured us out before now."

"Maybe they just saw something we were too blind to notice."

"Maybe."

He bent to kiss her. It started as a chaste good-night kiss, but once their lips touched, the chaste idea flew out the window. They were close to a repeat performance of what had happened in the living room when he backed away. "I think I'd better be going now," he whispered. She nodded and stepped away, letting him get through the door.

Jenny watched his car disappear down the street before she shut the front door. "Oh my, that was interesting," she said out loud. Disappointment mingled with relief, leaving her confused about her feelings. She was kind of glad he'd left, or she might have made a fool of herself. But she couldn't help wondering what it would have been like if he had stayed. The way she'd been acting, she wouldn't have made any effort to stop him. She knew it would have been a mistake, but she'd been playing it safe for too long. Throwing caution to the wind might have made for an interesting change of pace.

She stopped by the kitchen and poured herself a cup of coffee, looked at it for a second, then poured it out. She'd prefer to savor the taste of champagne and kisses on her lips and not sully it with coffee. She turned off the coffee pot, then, humming a bit of music from the concert, she waltzed to her bedroom, did a little spin, and came to a stop in front of the cheval mirror. She saw a woman in a rumpled silk dress, disheveled hair and swollen lips—a woman who looked absolutely ravishing, if she said so herself.

It was frightening, Jenny thought, how much her life had changed in that one night. She'd started the evening with plans of weaning herself from relying on Ken as her stand-by date. She'd ended the evening in a real relationship—if things worked out.

The usual fears and doubts nibbled at the back of her mind, warning her that things never seemed to work out and reminding her that she already knew what Ken was like. To shut off the overanalysis going on in her brain, she turned on the radio and started dancing around her bedroom to the slow love song that was playing. But Ken was right. Slow dancing just wasn't the same alone.

Now that she knew Ken, being alone wasn't the same, either. Where once she'd found solace, she now felt an emptiness, like she was missing part of herself. Had she weakened, or had she found the missing piece?

* * *

They'd probably kick him out of the brotherhood of guys for walking out of that situation, Ken thought to himself as he drove home. No man in his right mind would leave a woman who had been in his arms, responding to his every touch. But he was beginning to suspect that he wasn't in his right mind where Jenny Forrest was concerned. He was crazy—about her. And he didn't want to join the roster of ex-boyfriends she might someday run into at a wedding and try to hide from. Taking advantage of her tonight would have been a good way to put himself on the creep list.

He was not going to ruin this one. He was going to react sensibly and logically, not getting ahead of himself, and not panicking too early, either. He was ready. Kristen was a distant memory, so distant he wondered at the pain he'd felt over her loss. Now that he thought of it, that pain had faded as soon as he'd met Jenny.

Was this yet another of his headlong plunges into romance, or was it for real?

All he knew was he wanted this to be real, and he was going to do everything he could to make it so.

10

Ken felt as though he'd gone back in time a decade or so. He'd been in high school the last time he'd agonized so much over a phone call. Sunday he'd been tempted to call Jenny, just because he wanted to hear her voice, but he worried that he'd seem overeager and scare her off. He knew he was scaring himself. He'd never felt this way over anyone, not even Kristen. That had to mean this was more than his usual state of infatuation.

By Monday evening, he figured he'd waited long enough, and he could wait no longer. He had to talk to her, to know if she'd had second thoughts about stepping beyond their arrangement. As soon as he was confident she'd made it home from work and finished dinner, he dialed her number.

The phone rang several times, and he was mentally preparing a message to leave on her answering machine when she picked up. He fumbled for what to say for a second, caught between the greeting he'd originally planned and the hastily reworked answering machine greeting. "Uh, hi. It's me," he finally managed, and immediately wanted to bang his head against the wall for being so clumsy. At the rate he was going, his face was going to start breaking out at any second. "How are you?" he added, trying to recover his wits.

"I guess I'm okay," she said, sounding somewhat bewildered. He couldn't really blame her for that.

"Great. Uh, I was thinking of someplace to go to dinner Saturday, and I realized I don't know what kinds of food you like. I just know you don't like my father's hamburgers."

She chuckled. "Sorry, but you're right about that. I'm easy to please. About the only thing I don't like is seafood. I could go for whatever you like. And I don't know what you like, either."

This was feeling more and more like a first date to Ken, which was odd considering how much he did know about Jenny and how well he thought he knew her. "Funny, I don't like seafood either," he said.

"Then we've got at least one thing in common—other than pathetic social lives."

"It looks like we have a lot more to talk about than what we expect from a relationship."

"At least we won't have to worry about awkward silences. I hate it when that happens on a date, especially a first date. I start trying to fill the silence, and end up chattering."

Ken knew he needed to say something to avoid just such an awkward silence, but he couldn't think of anything. Mentally replaying the conversation to this point, he grasped at a topic. "Does steak sound good to you? There's a place downtown my parents love. I've never been there, but they talk about it all the time, so I'm sure it's got to be good."

"I don't eat steak often, but it sounds good to me."

"Great. I'll make reservations." Another silence. He decided to end this now while he was still relatively coherent. "Well, I guess I'll see you Saturday. I'm looking forward to it."

"So am I. And don't make plans for the next weekend. It could be our first nonemergency, nonstand-by date. A friend's getting married, and I'd like you to come with me."

"I guess we'll never get past those events, will we?"

"Not until all our friends and family are married, and we don't have to worry about office events anymore. Those are just a part of life."

"Don't worry, I'll be there again for you."

"Thanks. And I'll see you this weekend."

As soon as Ken hung up, dozens of witty conversational tidbits flooded his brain. He had to restrain himself from calling Jenny right back, just to show her what he was capable of. More than likely, he'd revert back to babbling idiot as soon as he heard her voice.

This was starting to feel frighteningly like love. And while he knew a lot about falling in love, Ken wasn't as clear on how to grow and build a love beyond the first burst of infatuation. He was entering new territory.

As the weekend grew nearer, Jenny grew more anxious about the date. She hadn't doubted Ken's sincerity in what he'd told her about his feelings Saturday night. But she also hadn't doubted his sincerity about his feelings for Kristen the night they met. From what she'd learned about him, he fell in love as often as most people did laundry, and he fell out just as often.

When she thought of it that way, she couldn't think why she'd accepted a real date with him. She'd accepted his quirks as a stand-by date who, by definition, wouldn't become serious. In a relationship, he might as well have had warning signs plastered all over him. Her past relationships had gone bad although she hadn't noticed anything glaringly wrong with the men from the start. She shuddered to think of what could happen with a man she knew to be dangerous.

But as long as she was aware of that, she didn't see what harm there could be in going out with Ken. And he'd probably get over her pretty quickly, once they actually had a "real" date or two. For now, though, she could enjoy herself. She'd just be on her guard. It would also feel good to quit putting on the couple act with her friends and his family. If this didn't work out, she doubted they'd go back to acting. Then they wouldn't have to pretend to break up.

He'd said they were going to a nice place—the kind that took reservations, which was becoming increasingly rare in an age of trendy chain restaurants that kept waiting lists instead of reservations. She didn't intend to go all out with her dress like she had the night of his dinner party or her concert, but she knew she should dress nicely. Saturday evening found her standing in front of her closet, trying to choose something. She'd deliberately put off the decision. Somehow, the date seemed more casual if she just threw something on instead of carefully planning.

It was almost time for Ken to pick her up when she finally just grabbed the blue dress she'd worn to her reunion, the night she first met Ken. Maybe it would bring back the magic of their first meeting, back when he was just a handsome stranger helping her pass the evening. At the time, she'd thought it was perfect as it was. Now she wondered if seeing him after that night had been such a good idea, after all.

Before she could completely overanalyze their situation, her doorbell rang. She slipped on her shoes and ran her hands over her hair before running to the door. When she opened it, she found herself face-to-face with Ken, dressed in that beautiful gray suit he'd worn to the wedding they'd gone to together. He handed her a single red rose as soon as she opened the door.

"Oh my," she said, taken aback. "Thank you." *Now, what?* she thought. "I guess I'd better put this in some water. Uh, please come in." He followed her to the kitchen, where she found a bud vase and filled it with water, then put the rose in it. A single red rose, she thought. Red stood for passion, and the single rose was supposed to signify eternal love. That was maybe a bit too much. She felt a chink develop in her emotional armor.

"I made reservations at that steak house downtown," he told her while she took care of the rose.

"Oh," she said, unable to think of anything more creative as the chink grew larger. She fought to rebuild the wall around her heart before she was left entirely unguarded.

"Ready?" he asked when she'd placed the vase in the center of her kitchen table.

"Sure," she said, picking up her purse from the counter.

"You look nice," he said, almost as an afterthought, as they walked to the car. "Isn't that the dress—"

"From the reunion," she finished his sentence, not sure if she should take that as criticism or a compliment.

"The night we met."

"You remembered?"

"I still remember exactly what you looked like when you came into that bar." He held the car door open for her as she got in.

"And what did I look like?" she asked when he had seated himself and started the engine.

"Like someone about to drink herself silly, and I was all ready to join you. Then you ordered a glass of wine."

"And that ruined the effect."

"That turned into a far more interesting evening. If we'd just sat there drinking, we wouldn't be where we are now."

"Where are we now?" she couldn't resist asking.

"Heading toward downtown," he replied with a wry smile.

He was really acting odd, she thought, more like a nervous first date than someone who'd been seeing her for more than a month.

Downtown at the restaurant, he let a valet park the car, then the maître d' escorted them to their table. The heavy furniture, candlelight and elegant atmosphere created an intimate mood that made Jenny uneasy. All around them were couples who were very obviously couples. For the first time with Ken, she felt conscious of the fact that no matter what everyone else thought about them, they really weren't a pair. This truly was their first date, the first time since they'd met that they had come together because they were Jenny and Ken, not anyone else's friend or family member and significant other.

"What about an appetizer?" he asked, looking over the top of his menu at her.

"Sure," she said.

"Let's see, I guess we don't want the shrimp cocktail," he said with a smile.

"Oh, yeah, neither of us likes seafood." That was one of the few things she knew about him, other than who his parents were, his recent romantic history and some of his hopes and fears.

"Stuffed mushrooms?"

"Sounds good."

"And we may as well get a bottle of wine. Probably a red, unless you think you'll get something other than steak."

"That should work." At least he wasn't ordering champagne. That would have been a complete overkill.

The waiter came to their table, and Ken ordered the appetizer and wine. Then they returned to studying the main courses on the menu. When the waiter returned with their wine, they both ordered steaks and potatoes.

The ordering done, they were left alone together to talk, with no clear cue on a topic. It hadn't been this hard the night they first met.

"We've come a long way," he said, raising his glass in a sort of toast.

Yeah, from intimate strangers to this awkward arrangement, she thought, but out loud she said, "Yes, we have," and she clinked her glass lightly against his. This was a bad idea, a very bad idea, she thought as her uneasiness grew stronger. She should have listened to her instincts and refused to see him again. At least then she would have had the memory of that one perfect evening when she'd expected nothing and come away with something magical.

The waiter brought their appetizer, and Jenny was glad to be able to concentrate on stuffing mushrooms into her mouth rather than trying to think of something to say to Ken. What had they talked about that first time, back when the conversation had flowed so easily? Oh yeah, they'd talked about the disappointments in their lives that had led them where they were at that moment. On second thought, maybe that wasn't a good starting point.

"So, how was your week?" Ken finally asked.

"Good. You?"

"Pretty good. Busy. My mom asked after you."

"Oh, really?" Then she laughed and shook her head. "Listen to us. We sound like total strangers on a blind date."

"At least we're not talking about the weather."

"I'm afraid that would be more interesting than, 'How was your week?'"

"True. Especially in Texas."

"Yeah, this has to be one of the rare places where the weather is actually an interesting topic."

Then he laughed. "We're doing it, aren't we."

"Yes, we're talking about the weather," she replied with a smile.

"I believe we've now officially sunk to the depths of a boring date."

"I bet no one who's seen us together over the last month or so would believe we could be like this once we're alone."

"I thought you were uncomfortable with the act we were putting on."

"It wasn't the acting itself that bothered me so much," she said, staring at the damp ring her water glass was leaving on the tablecloth. "I'd just prefer it if everyone wasn't so excited about us dating that they're practically planning the wedding. I've found that the longer you let a lie or a misperception survive, the worse it gets when the truth comes out. I'm just not comfortable with a pretend relationship."

"I'm not so thrilled about acting, either," he said after a pause. Then he grinned, "But we must be good at it. Everyone is convinced that we're a really hot item."

She laughed. "I'll be looking for this year's Oscar nominations. We're sure to be on the list." This was more like it, she thought. They'd relaxed a bit, now that the funny feeling of being on a date with no ulterior purpose had worn off. Maybe all her fears had been unfounded.

The waiter arrived with their meal, and conversation became a distraction as they concentrated on thick, juicy steaks and buttered potatoes. It was enough to rhapsodize over the food. Jenny knew she'd have to walk miles to work off the meal, but it was worth it.

But after the waiter cleared their plates and had taken their dessert order, Ken resumed the earlier conversation, with a much more serious tone. "These last couple of months have been fun," he said.

"Yeah, they have. I'd forgotten what it was like to leave the house every so often."

"I'm glad I met you," he continued. "You were just what I needed to find at this stage in my life."

He sounded a bit too serious, and Jenny's nerves went on alert. If he hadn't been so concerned about defining this as a "real" date, she would swear she was about to get dumped. This sounded too much like the nice things men tried to say to ease the parting blow.

She was about to say something to lighten things up when she was distracted by a new group of patrons being led to their table. "Ken?" she said, trying to keep her expression neutral.

"What is it?"

"Remember how you said your parents really liked this place?"

"Yeah, they come here often. Why?"

"Well, don't look now, but they just came in."

He started to turn around, but she stopped him with a quick kick on the ankle. "I said, don't look."

"Have they noticed us?"

"Not yet."

"I didn't say anything about coming here. I didn't even talk to them this week."

"If they see us here, you know what they'll think."

"What?"

Before she could answer, she had to school her features into a friendly smile as the Parkses approached their table. Ken noticed her expression and turned just in time to greet his parents.

"What on earth are you two doing here?" Ellen asked. "This wouldn't be a special occasion, now, would it?"

Ken raised an eyebrow. "You never know," he said with a grin and a wink at Jenny.

Ken's parents exchanged glances. "Why didn't you tell us you had something planned for tonight?" Ellen asked. "We wouldn't have intruded on your evening if we'd known."

"I figured the odds were against both of us being here on the same night. Looks like I was wrong."

"Then I guess we'd better leave you two alone for a while." She patted Jenny on the shoulder. "It's good to see you again, Jenny. I hope we'll be seeing a lot more of you in the future." With a sly wink over her shoulder at Ken, she herded her husband back to their table.

Jenny groaned as soon as they were out of earshot. "Oh, boy," she said.

"What?"

"You know what they're bound to be thinking about us."

He glanced across the room toward his parents, who seemed to be studying the younger couple over the tops of their menus. "They'll know we're still 'together.' And that it's kind of serious if I'm taking you here."

She shook her head. "Are you really that dense? People don't just come to this place because they're hungry. This is the kind of place you go for anniversaries—or engagements."

His jaw dropped. Then he shook his head. "No, my parents come here all the time. They won't think anything of it."

"Have you taken a woman here before?"

"I've never even been here before. This isn't the kind of place I usually take dates."

"Exactly. And with the way your mother's mind works, you know what she's got to be thinking. She thinks they'll be ordering champagne at the end of the evening."

He ran his hands over his face. "Jenny, I'm sorry. I guess I didn't think. I was just trying to come as close as I could to the way you described your ideal real date. I never expected us to have an audience."

She patted his hand where it rested on the table, then quickly withdrew her hand, conscious of the Parkses' watching eyes. "Don't worry. I don't suspect you of setting me up. But we've got to be careful how we act tonight, or they really will be thinking things."

"They'll be disappointed if they get their hopes up too high."

"I'm tired of playing games, Ken. We've been acting the whole time we've been together. I'm not even sure what I really feel about you, or about us."

"Yeah, I've been thinking a lot about that lately," he said. "I really wish I could figure it all out. The last time I had someone really special in my life, I let her go because I couldn't make a decision. I don't intend to let that happen again."

"That's probably a good policy," she agreed. "But you live and you learn from your past mistakes."

He traced an unseen pattern on the tablecloth with one finger. "But I think I was right about that decision, after all," he said, watching the tablecloth rather than looking at her. "I used to think I'd made an emotional decision that wasn't a wise one. Since then, I've learned that sometimes the heart can be smarter than the brain."

Jenny frowned, uncomfortable with the direction the conversation was going. Just a few minutes ago, they were talking about how little they really knew each other. Now here Ken was, sounding even more intimate than he had the night they met. "I'm not sure what you're saying here. Do you mean all that moaning over Kristen was nothing? You've decided now that you weren't so crazy about her?" Her emotional alarm system went to red alert. She'd already dealt with one guy who practiced revisionist romantic history. She didn't need another. Who knew what he'd think about her a few months down the line, depending on whether his heart or his head was talking.

"I guess what I'm saying, Jenny, is I'm glad I didn't end up with Kristen because that would have meant I wouldn't have had a chance with you. I don't want to make the same mistake twice. I don't want to risk losing you."

He reached across the table and took her hand. "That's why I wanted to make tonight special. I wanted to start out right. Who knows where it could lead from here?"

She shook her head wordlessly. "Wow!" she said when she finally found her voice. "I thought this was a first date."

"I don't think we can pretend that nothing's ever happened between us. I think we've both felt it. We'll just have to make up our own rules as we go."

Closing her eyes and taking a deep breath, she clasped his hand, then opened her eyes and gave him a smile. "Okay. But no more games."

"No more games," he agreed. "And I can take you for a burger next week to make up for tonight. I guess I got a little overly enthusiastic."

She chuckled. "Normally I don't complain about that sort of thing. It's just that I didn't want your parents to get yet another wrong impression about us. It's bad enough that they're going to think we've got the slowest-moving relationship in history, since they think we've been working on it for a while already."

"Someday we'll be laughing about this."

He looked a little too serious about that. His gray eyes never left her face as he spoke. The only thing that broke the spell was the arrival of the waiter with a bottle of champagne. "Compliments of some of our other patrons, with their congratulations," he said.

"What?" Jenny and Ken said at the same time, then they both turned to see Ken's parents staring at them.

"No, oh no," Jenny murmured.

"Obviously, they got the wrong impression," Ken said, in a great understatement.

Jenny mentally replayed the past few minutes. Ken had taken her hand and said something serious. She'd closed her eyes in thought, then smiled at him and clasped his hand. "They think we just got engaged," she whispered.

"I think this situation just got very interesting."

"We've got to explain it to them. We'll have to come clean with the whole story," she insisted. "I knew we were bound to get caught sooner or later."

"We don't have to tell it all. We can just tell them there's no ring, yet."

She shook her head. "No. We just said no games. We're in this situation now because we've kept playing games. I don't intend to continue it any longer. If this is going to be for real, let's be real." She felt the room closing in on her as her panic rose. She should have known nothing good could have come out of this. It was time to cut her losses and get out of here, fast, before she fell further under the spell of those intense gray eyes.

"Who says it isn't real? It's perfectly honest to say there's no ring yet."

"Are you already assuming that's where we're going to end up, though? What are you going to say if there's never a ring, if this doesn't work out? At some point in your life, Ken, you're going to have to quit playing games and be real about something." She took her purse from where it hung on the back of her chair and stood. "Well, this game is now over. You've been wondering how you were going to tell your parents we weren't an item. I think they'll figure it out now."

Then she turned and purposefully strode toward the exit, hoping her wobbling legs would carry her. On her way, she passed their waiter, who was carrying two slices of cherry cheesecake on a tray—their dessert. "Could I get mine boxed to go?" she asked.

He blinked, then assured her he would take care of it, as if he got this kind of request every day. That was the good thing about nice restaurants; their staff was trained to handle the weirdest whims without comment. She went on to the maître d' and asked him to call her a cab. Just before her cab arrived, the waiter brought her a small box. She climbed into the back seat of the cab, cradling her box. After what she had just gone through emotionally, she couldn't have passed up the cheesecake.

As the cab pulled away from the restaurant, the tears she'd been fighting to hold back began trickling down her cheeks. She wiped them away angrily. She should have known better. He'd been trouble from the start. But what was one broken heart more. At least she had the cheesecake. It wasn't a total loss.

11

Ken was so stunned, he was frozen, unable to move and unsure if he should move. He couldn't tell if Jenny had really been that upset, or if she had staged that display for his parents' benefit. He could feel his parents' eyes on him. With any luck, they would be too embarrassed to approach him, so he could delay that particular humiliation.

While he sat at the table, staring at the door where Jenny had disappeared and trying to decide if he should go after her or not, the waiter approached with a tray bearing two slices of cheesecake. The waiter placed one slice on the table in front of Ken, then said, "The lady will have hers to go." He disappeared, carrying the other slice.

Despite the awkwardness of his situation, Ken couldn't help smiling. That was so like Jenny, and one of the reasons he'd fallen for her. Leave it to Jenny Forrest to have the presence of mind to make sure she still got her dessert, even after a heartbreaking, emotional scene. It reminded him of the night he met her, when she was able to make witty conversation even as she fought back tears.

He toyed with his dessert, but had no appetite left. His brain was too busy rerunning the last few minutes of their conversation. If he had tried, he couldn't have handled it any worse. It wasn't all his parents' fault; in fact, he couldn't blame them at all. If he hadn't been afraid to admit to them the way he'd felt about Kristen and how he'd met Jenny, this never would have turned out the way it had. They would have understood. They probably would have had a good laugh over the revelation that he barely knew the lovely young woman he'd brought to the picnic.

He wasn't even sure why the truth had been so hard to tell. Could it be because, even then, he wished the game had been the truth, and if they acted the role of lovers often enough, it might become real?

The waiter paused at his table again. "I think I'll have my dessert to go, too," Ken told him. "Could you please deliver the champagne to that couple over there—" he indicated his parents "—with my compliments. And I'd like the check, please."

The waiter whisked away the uneaten cheesecake and carried the champagne bucket over to the Parkses. Ken glanced in their direction and gave them a little salute. They looked shocked, as well they should. He owed them an explanation, but first he had something to take care of.

The waiter returned with a small box and the check. Ken handed over his credit card, then drummed his fingers on the table while he waited for the man to return with the credit card slip. He scribbled his signature as soon as it was placed on the table, then he grabbed his box of cheesecake and left the dining room.

There was no sign of Jenny in the vestibule, so he went outside and looked up and down the street. All he saw were couples walking arm in arm down the sidewalk. No Jenny. So, she hadn't just been staging a public breakup for his parents' benefit to keep them from suspecting an engagement. She had been really upset, and probably hurt.

Ken groaned and leaned against the brick wall of the restaurant. All his promises to himself and to her friends, and he'd hurt her anyway. He'd been so busy keeping himself from getting hurt that he hadn't seen what he was doing to her with his little games. The last time he'd been in love—or thought he was—he'd messed up by letting the girl go before realizing his feelings. This time he'd messed up by not being aware of anyone's feelings—his or Jenny's. No matter what he did, he just seemed to keep losing. Someday maybe he'd get it right, but he had hoped it would be with Jenny.

Ken shoved himself away from the wall and trudged back into the restaurant. "The lady who was with me?" he asked.

The maître d' looked up at him and said, "She took a cab."

"Thanks," Ken nodded, then went back outside and had the valet retrieve his car. He just hoped Jenny would talk to him when he got there.

Jenny slammed the front door behind her and kicked her shoes across the hallway. She wasn't sure if she was mad at herself or at Ken. She knew their act was going to get them in trouble, and she'd been right. She could play make-believe girlfriend, but she wasn't going to pretend to be engaged to anyone, and she wasn't going to let herself fall into that kind of situation by default. She wanted to know for sure where Ken stood before going that far, and from what she'd seen, his feelings changed as rapidly as the North Texas weather. She'd been foolish to let her own feelings get out of control before being sure of his. Someday she'd learn that lesson.

She carried her cheesecake into the kitchen and poured herself a glass of milk. She nibbled absently at the cheesecake, already regretting her actions at the restaurant. Ken hadn't deserved the public humiliation she'd given him, no matter how much he'd set them up for such a situation. She didn't think they could continue as they had before, and she wasn't sure she could trust him enough to move into a so-called real relationship, but she did owe him an apology.

Putting down her fork, Jenny reached for the phone, but hesitated before picking it up. Her hand trembled. She wanted more than anything to call Ken to come to her. To have him take her in his arms and kiss her and say the wonderful, romantic things she knew he was capable of saying to her. It would be a memorable night. The problem came in what might happen a week, maybe a month, maybe a year later, when he changed his mind and decided that she wasn't right for him and someone else was.

It was about time she learned from her mistakes, Jenny told herself. This had happened to her before. Ken hadn't seen a pattern in her pitiful romantic history, but now it became perfectly clear to her. She'd always let herself get emotionally involved before being totally sure where she stood. Well, this time, she knew all too well where she stood—on romantic quicksand. She withdrew her hand and turned her back on the phone. She could call him later, when she was a little more emotionally steady.

But she wasn't allowed to be alone with her thoughts for long. The doorbell rang, and Jenny knew who it had to be. She couldn't pretend not to be home, not after the way she'd just treated him. If she was going to apologize, she could have the guts to do it to his face. She shoved her cheesecake aside and went to answer the door.

Just as she had suspected, a very contrite-looking Ken stood on her doorstep. Before she could say anything, he said, "I'm sorry. You were right. I shouldn't have let us get into that kind of situation. I should have told my parents the truth earlier." His eyes were focused on the toes of his shoes, making him look for all the world like a schoolboy caught in a prank. Then he looked up at her and his mouth twitched into a slight smile. "I guess I just didn't want to break their hearts. They liked you so much, I knew they'd never forgive me for letting someone like you go, or for only pretending to date you. And I hated to tell them what had really happened with Kristen."

"I'm sorry, too. I guess I could have handled that a little better than I did. I hope I didn't leave you with too many awkward explanations to make." She felt even worse now about what she'd done, not just for Ken's sake, but also for his parents.

"I haven't explained yet. I'll talk to them later. I just hope they enjoyed the champagne."

"As long as someone did. The cheesecake was pretty good."

He grinned briefly. "I'm glad you liked it. I'll have mine when I get home."

They stood looking at each other for a moment, then Jenny realized this conversation was taking place on her doorstep. Even though she wasn't sure it was a good idea, she stepped back from the door. "Why don't you come in?" she said.

He paused, then said, "I guess we do need to talk," before stepping through the doorway.

She guided him to the living room, then gestured for him to take a seat on the sofa. She sat on the opposite end, facing him. He sat facing straight ahead, his back straight and his shoulders tense.

"Okay, so what exactly is going on with us?" she asked. "I can't play games anymore. I need to know where you stand, and I need to know where I stand with you." He remained staring straight ahead, his hands resting on his knees. She ran a hand through her hair in frustration and was shocked to notice that her hand trembled. She'd never dared ask a man point-blank where she stood with him, and now she feared his answer. "Was this all a game for you, or did you mean what you said tonight? Is this at all real?"

"I think this is real," he said softly, turning his head to look at her.

"And I remember you thinking Kristen was real. I don't want to go on as some kind of consolation prize or honorable mention, someone to keep you from feeling too bad because you screwed up once before, or someone you grab on to because you're afraid of going it alone and you know I'm available." And she knew she couldn't take it if he decided later that maybe he'd been wrong about her, too.

"Okay, so maybe this was all bad timing. We let things get too far before coming clean with each other," Ken admitted.

"Just because the first date was on an emergency stand-by basis didn't mean we had to continue that way if we both felt something more."

"But what if we both didn't?" Ken asked. "I didn't want to say anything to you because after all your talk of safe dates, I was worried you wanted a safe date more than you wanted someone who was interested in you. If I said something and you didn't feel the same way, I wouldn't even be a good emergency date anymore."

"I think after last weekend, you had a pretty good idea where I stood on that." She studied him for a moment, then said, "It's all or nothing with you, isn't it?"

"What do you mean by that?"

"You're head over heels, or else completely over someone. Once you're interested, you might as well call the preacher and book the church. And that's not the way I work. I don't want to have to wonder whether you're going to have another revelation and realize maybe I'm not right for you, after all."

He caught her in his dark gray gaze and said softly, his voice hoarse with emotion, "Someday you're going to learn that you have to take a few risks in life. There aren't any guarantees. But if you aren't willing to take a chance for fear of being hurt, you'll end up alone."

"There's nothing wrong with being alone," she said, fighting to keep her dignity although his words stung badly enough to bring tears to her eyes. "But it would be hell to always wonder where I stood with you." She shrugged and added, "Maybe I will get a cat."

He rose from the sofa. "Well, then, I guess we don't have much more to talk about. I'd better be going. I can find my own way out."

She closed her eyes as she heard the front door slam. If she'd turned him away because she didn't want to be hurt, why was she in so much pain now?

Ken leaned over the sink, eating his cheesecake, even though it tasted like cardboard. He was sure it tasted much better under normal circumstances, but all his senses seemed to have gone numb. After starting the evening in high hopes, he now felt pretty bleak.

Unfortunately, he couldn't think of anything he could do to improve matters. Anything he tried was only going to scare Jenny even more. He was going to have to earn her trust. To do that would require being around her, which would, in turn, require earning her trust. No matter which way he looked at it, he was pretty much stuck.

He didn't think this was the right time for a grand romantic gesture, like serenading her beneath her bedroom window. She'd probably call the cops if he tried that. Flowers delivered to her office would just seem desperate and make it look like he was trying to buy her affection.

What he needed was a good reason to be around her, to show her as best he could what he really felt, to reassure her that he wasn't going to hurt her like all those others—all her frogs—had before. Something like...like the wedding next weekend.

He laughed out loud as he remembered that he'd already accepted her invitation to her friend's wedding. She couldn't back out now. She might consider this their very last emergency stand-by date, but she'd let him go, he was sure of it. Now he just had to think of how to remind her, or maybe he should just show up.

And he had a week to think of what he'd do when he got her there.

Jenny didn't think all this macaroni and cheese could possibly be good for her, but she didn't feel like waiting for anything to be delivered, and she certainly didn't want to go out to pick something up. Someday she'd have to learn to cook something else.

She'd come home from work the past couple of days

half hoping, half dreading to find a message on her answering machine. Then she spent the evening half hoping, half dreading that the phone would ring. She didn't know what she'd say if Ken did call, but she wanted to hear his voice, to know if he was okay.

"There you go, getting all dependent again," she muttered to herself as she dropped her fork in the sink and returned the pan of macaroni and cheese to the refrigerator. She thought she'd outgrown this kind of clinginess years ago. "My happiness doesn't depend on a man," she declared to one of her houseplants. Its leaves were yellowing, she noticed. Maybe it needed water.

Opening the cabinet under the sink, she rummaged for the watering can. When the phone rang, she hit her head on the counter, she jumped up so quickly. She forced herself to wait for two rings before picking the phone up. A hard knot grew in her stomach as she said, "Hello?" If it was Ken, she'd panic. If it wasn't, she'd probably cry, despite her best intentions.

It wasn't Ken. It was Sharon. "Hey, Jen, I was just checking to see if you were going to be at Karen's wedding this weekend. Amy isn't going to be able to go, so I wanted to see if anyone else I know will be there."

Karen's wedding? Jenny took a quick glance at the calendar on the refrigerator door, then had to stifle a groan as she remembered. "Yeah, I was planning to be there," she said, wishing she could come up with an excuse not to be there. She'd already responded, and it would be rude to back out now.

"Great! I guess Ken will be there, too."

She'd already asked him, and she'd responded for both of them. At the time, it had felt good to have an "and guest" to invite. Now being the third wheel with Sharon and Jack sounded like a better idea. "Yeah, he's planning on it. I hope he can still make it. He may have to work." She might as well start working on an excuse now. The way he'd looked when he left Saturday night, he didn't seem open for emergency stand-by dates.

"I'll see you two then. And you'll have to let me know what you've been up to."

Jenny said goodbye, then hung up the phone and buried her face in her hands. She was going to have to swallow her pride and confirm the invitation, even though a wedding was the last place she wanted to be with Ken right now.

Before her courage could fail her, she picked up the phone and dialed his number, then prayed for an answering machine to pick up so she could just leave a message. Then it would be up to him to call her back.

No such luck. He answered the phone. Wincing, she said, "Hi. It's Jenny."

"Hi," he replied, sounding surprised.

"Uh, remember that wedding I invited you to, for this weekend?"

"Yeah."

She took a deep breath and plunged in. "Are you still going to be able to make it? I responded for the two of us, and I just needed to see if you would still go. I hate to show up on my own after responding for two, and I don't think I can find another date at this short notice. This would be a real emergency stand-by thing, nothing more."

"Of course I'll go," he said. "I couldn't back out on you."

She was sure her sigh of relief was audible, even over the phone. "Great. I'm glad. So, I'll see you Saturday at six?"

"Saturday at six, it is."

"Thank you, Ken. I appreciate this."

"Take care, Jenny." He hung up before she could say anything in reply.

She put the phone back on its cradle, then bent over the counter, resting her head on her folded arms. Just one more date wouldn't hurt. Then she could go back to her ordinary life, without all the ups, downs and complications that came with men. Just her and her plants—if the plants survived.

She just wondered where she'd find another good stand-by date after this was over. She'd become accustomed to having someone to invite. It would be hard to return to going alone.

On his way to Jenny's house Saturday evening, Ken rehearsed his strategy. He'd be friendly, but not showing so much interest that it would make her nervous. Then, when she had relaxed enough to listen to him, he'd talk to her. He wouldn't expect a commitment now, just the chance to see what they could develop together. The fact that she'd been the one to call him about the wedding was a good sign. He might just stand a chance.

As he pulled up in front of her house, the butterflies in his stomach went berserk, brilliant plan or not. This was his final chance to make things right with her, and he couldn't afford to ruin it.

It took her a minute or two to open the door after he rang the bell, and when he saw her, he immediately thought of the night they'd met. Now, as then, she gave every indication of fighting to hold back extreme emotion. Her back was straight and stiff, her shoulders were tense, her head was held high and her chin jutted forward defiantly.

"Hi, Jenny, how are you?" he said, making no move

to touch her or kiss her, even though he wanted nothing more than to throw his arms around her and hold her close.

"I'm doing okay," she said. She glanced down at the ground, pushed a lock of hair behind her ear, then added softly, "I'm sorry again about last weekend. I hope your parents weren't too hard on you."

"It wasn't too bad. My mom's disappointed. She really likes you. And I got no end of grief for not being honest with them all along. They thought our arrangement was kind of amusing."

She looked up at him and the beginnings of a smile teased at her lips. "It does make for a good story, doesn't it? My mom enjoyed it," she said, a little of her usual light sparking in her eyes.

The butterflies in Ken's stomach calmed down a bit. This was going far better than he'd expected. She was at least talking to him relatively normally. "Are you ready?" he asked.

"Yeah." She locked the front door and walked with him to the car.

Jenny was silent for the first part of the trip, but he didn't try to force conversation. He didn't want to push his luck. As they neared the church, she cleared her throat. "I think I should warn you that a lot of the people here today will have been at that other wedding. Sharon and Jack will be there, too."

"And they think we're a hot item," he said, completing her thought.

"Yeah, but we don't have to put on the couple act. In fact, it would probably be a good thing if we do appear a bit distant. That would make it more believable when we don't show up together the next time."

He nodded and tried not to let her statement get to

him. She still seemed to be of the opinion that this was the last time they'd be together.

After another silence, she said, "I really appreciate this, Ken. You've saved my life once again."

"No problem. Glad to help. That's what a stand-by date is all about."

"There's one more thing I should tell you," she said a moment later. "The reception's in the same hotel as the last wedding we went to." She didn't have to add that it was also the place they'd met. They'd come full circle. Tonight was going to be either an ending or another beginning.

12

Although she'd started the evening apprehensive, by the time they got to the hotel for the reception, Jenny had almost managed to forget what had come between her and Ken. This felt like old times. The wedding had been formal, long and terribly romantic. Jenny had found herself fighting back tears as the soloists sang of eternal love. It was almost enough to make her rethink her stance on being single.

The hotel ballroom was crowded, forcing Jenny to clutch Ken's elbow to keep from being separated from him. Even though she was among people she knew, she was glad she wasn't here alone. Crowds like this tended to make her feel invisible. Ken was a solid anchor that made her feel steady and secure.

They'd barely made it through the doorway when Sharon found them. She hugged both of them, startling Ken, and gave Jenny a kiss on the cheek. "Jenny! It's good to see you again," she said. "I notice you're still with this guy. I've got to go find Jack. I'll catch you two later." With a wink at Ken, she gave Jenny an encouraging pat on the shoulder, then disappeared back into the crowd.

Jenny groaned. "I guess we need to plan yet another breakup, this time for the benefit of my friends."

"Why don't we do that one offstage this time?" he said with a wry grin, squeezing her arm. She shivered at the touch as it reminded her that she still stood arm in arm with him.

"You don't have to keep this act going tonight," she whispered. "No one but Sharon will really notice."

She turned out to be wrong about that assumption. Several guests greeted them as they moved through the room. Many had been at the last wedding they'd gone to together, and everyone seemed to remember the fact that Ken had caught the garter. They took the fact that Jenny and Ken were still together as proof that the old superstition was valid. The more people they talked to, the more Jenny and Ken fell into their old routine of playing a couple. It was easier to act than to explain the situation.

"You know, you were right," Ken murmured to Jenny as they took a break from the mingling to get some punch.

"I'm right about a lot of things," she said, raising one eyebrow at him. "What is it this time?"

"The way people—particularly couples—look at singles. If either of us were here alone, we'd be getting all sorts of lectures about not being married yet. But with us together, everyone seems to think our lives are wonderful, like being part of a couple is all it takes to make your life complete."

"I believe that only works if you've found the person who completes you."

"And that's not so easy to do."

"Maybe once in a lifetime," she agreed.

"The trick is knowing when you've found it."

That was the trick, wasn't it? But how was she supposed to figure out which was the once-in-a-lifetime love, and which was yet another frog?

"And you have to be sure," she murmured.

"There are no guarantees, Jen. Sometimes you just have to go with your instincts."

This conversation was suddenly getting way too personal. Jenny looked up, and for once, was glad to see Sharon heading back in their direction, dragging Jack behind her. "Don't look now," she whispered.

"She's never going to give up until she sees us walk down the aisle," Ken muttered.

"I'll tell her the whole story sometime this week. Don't worry. You won't have to go through this again. You don't even have to keep pretending now."

"No problem. Like I said, we can do the break-up scene offstage. Let her feel good for now." He put on a grin just as Sharon and Jack worked their way through the crowd.

"Boy, am I glad you two are here. This place is a zoo," Sharon gasped. "Everyone here looks kind of familiar, but I don't think I know anyone well enough to talk to them."

"Funny, everyone seems to remember us well enough to talk to us," Jenny said ruefully.

"Let's face it, honey, you two put on quite a show at the last wedding. People remember that kind of thing. They're waiting to see if you'll be next."

Jenny felt her cheeks grow warm. She felt even worse now about having deceived her friends. It was going to be hard to come clean, but it would be worse to pretend a breakup. Knowing Sharon and Amy, her friends would move heaven and earth to try to get them back together again.

Ken didn't seem to be feeling the same pressure. He just smiled at Sharon and said, "You never know."

Sharon tilted her head to one side and asked, "Does that mean we'll be hearing something soon?"

He slipped his arm around Jenny's shoulders and said, "Very likely."

Sharon beamed, then said, "Good." She exchanged looks with Jack. "I think we're going to forage for a while. We'll be watching when they toss the bouquet."

Jenny let her breath out with a deep sigh as soon as the others were out of earshot. "Gee, thanks. Now you've made it even harder for me," she said.

"I didn't say anything. She took it the way she wanted to take it."

"But you managed to be awfully convincing. I just wish I could believe you as easily as everyone else does. But you're just too good an actor, aren't you? Do you ever stop acting?"

"How do you know I'm acting?"

"I never know."

"Just because I've been a jerk doesn't mean that's all I am all the time. Has it crossed your mind that I might mean what I say about you?"

She studied his face, searching for some clue of what he really felt, but she was afraid the answer lay more within her than with him. "I'm sure you mean it—for now," she said after a while. "I'm just not sure that you know how you really feel."

He sighed. "We need to talk. One way or another, we've got to resolve this. I don't want to lose you as a friend, and if we keep on like this, I'm afraid that's what will happen."

She glanced around the crowded ballroom, filled with laughing, talking wedding guests. The dance band was going full force, adding to the chaos. "I don't think this is the place to talk," she pointed out.

"I think I know a quiet place around here that's good for talking."

She didn't have to ask where he meant. She simply took his hand and let him lead her out of the ballroom and down to the lounge where they'd met.

They settled into the seats where they'd spent an evening telling each other their deepest feelings. "We've got to stop meeting like this," Ken quipped.

A waitress came by to take their order. "The lady will have a glass of white zinfandel," Ken said, then grinned and said, "and so will I." When the waitress left, he shrugged and said, "I thought I might as well give it a try."

"Maybe I should have ordered a rum and cola, then," Jenny said with a smile. For a conversation she'd been dreading, this was going well, so far.

He shifted in his seat and cleared his throat. "Let's do this like we did when we first met, listening to each other without trying to judge. Then you can say what you want to say. And no running out before I'm through. Agreed?"

She nodded. "Agreed. And I'm sorry for running out on you before."

"What did I say?" he asked, shaking a finger at her. "This is my turn."

"Okay," she said, properly chastened.

He laced his fingers together and popped his knuckles, then took a deep breath and said, "First of all, I don't think I was ever totally honest with you, even at the beginning. What I told you made me sound like a jerk who was afraid of commitment."

Frowning, he scratched the back of his neck and

paused as if in thought before continuing. "Truth is, I'm a hopeless romantic. I fall hard and fast, before I've had a chance to think things through. I'm also an idealist. I know there's someone out there for me, someone who will complete me." He laughed softly, then smiled. "It sounds silly, but I want to hear music—violins, bells, the whole orchestra. I've had a bad habit of moving on when I don't think I hear the music.

"That's why I broke up with Kristen. My head was telling me to stick it out with her. She was comfortable. But I didn't hear the music, and I couldn't make myself settle for less. When I saw her walk down the aisle, I thought I heard the music, if I strained hard enough."

"That was the Wedding March," Jenny remarked, smiling. It was hard to imagine Ken as a foolish romantic, but she was starting to get the picture.

He chuckled. "I know that, now. But I think seeing her in the wedding dress, knowing I had burned that particular bridge, scared me a bit. I didn't want to ever risk losing someone important over some silly romantic notion. What if I never heard violins? So, there I was, sitting in that bar, swearing to myself I wouldn't be like that anymore, that I was going to take a break from romance, and then I was going to think first. Then you walked in."

Turning to face her directly, he took her hands in both of his. "And then, Jenny, I heard the music."

Jenny had to swallow hard to clear the lump that had grown in her throat. "What kind of music was it?" she asked, struggling for a light tone.

His eyes grew unfocused as he thought, then he smiled and said, "It turned out I was wrong about the violins. What I heard was a slow, sultry saxophone. Does that sound right?"

"I suppose so." She'd never put much thought into what kind of music should go with a momentous occasion in life. It wasn't as if real life came complete with a sound track, like a movie. Although she did recall a saxophone that night... "But Ken, if you felt that way, why all the stand-by date stuff?"

"That's what I keep asking myself," he said, shaking his head. "I was trying so hard to mend my ways, and I was afraid I was just on the rebound, hearing music everywhere I went. I considered it a real triumph that I let you get away that night without making plans to see you again."

"But you took the name tag."

"I guess I wasn't as cured as I thought. And at first, I did try to stick to your stand-by date rules. That seemed to be just what I needed. Then I kissed you at the picnic, and it became a lot more difficult. The more time we spent together, the more I kept slipping back to my old ways."

She nodded and licked her lips. Looking back at all that had happened with this in mind, suddenly everything made so much more sense. No wonder she'd been so confused.

He squeezed the hand he still held. "I never wanted to hurt you, Jenny. That's why it took so long for me to say or do anything. You'd told me what you'd been through, and I couldn't do that to you. I kept thinking I'd get over you, that maybe it was just another phase I was going through."

"But it's not, is it?" she whispered.

"I don't think so."

She looked down at their joined hands and rubbed her thumb lightly across his knuckles. Her brain struggled to process all she'd just heard.

After several minutes of silence, he prodded gently, "Jenny? It's your turn now."

"I'm still thinking. I don't know what to think." She shook her head, as if to clear it.

"Take your time."

She laughed softly. "You know, all those things I said to you were true. I was so happy being single. It felt good to know I didn't need anybody else to make me feel complete. That's why I hated social events so much. They seemed designed to take that happiness away from me. It was like I was breaking the rules, and I deserved to be punished."

Looking up, she found herself staring into his dark eyes. They were fixed intently on her face, as if his whole future were being decided in her next words. She took a shaky breath and said, "Then I met you, and all those events I used to hate became fun. That was great. But the more time we spent together, the less happy I was alone. I hated that. I really did. I felt like it made me weak, like I was growing dependent."

"There's nothing wrong with needing someone else."

"But every time I've let myself get that way, it all falls down around me."

"Then how do you expect to ever find happiness? Can you tell me that, Jenny?" There was a harsh edge to his voice. "Sometimes you just have to trust and take a chance."

She looked down at her lap. "I just don't know. It's a big step for me."

He laughed and placed both hands on her shoulders, forcing her to look squarely at him. "Jenny, dear, I'm not asking you to commit your life to me right now. I do feel that way about you, and I don't think it's going to change, but I'm not asking you to take any giant leaps."

"What do you want me to say?" she whispered, searching his face and seeing the love there.

"I want you to give us a chance, to see what happens when we get together as Ken and Jenny, not as stand-by dates."

"We could still go to weddings and office parties together, though?" she asked with a smile.

"Most definitely, but as real significant others, not as stand-by dates."

"It seems kind of odd going back to square one after all we've been through together. The night we met, we learned more about each other than I've known about my last three boyfriends put together."

"Then we know a lot of what to expect. We know what to look out for."

"So, where and how do we go about this starting over business?"

"I think we're in the right place for it," he said, gesturing around the hotel bar. "Why don't we indulge in a little time travel. I'm sitting here alone and down in the dumps. You walk in, equally down in the dumps, and I hear music. I ask you what's wrong, we talk, we dance a little."

He stood and extended a hand to her. "Why don't we dance a little?"

She took his hand and let him pull her to her feet. "As I recall, it was a slow dance," he said, his voice soft and warm in her ear. He pulled her next to him, and she allowed her body to melt against his. She remembered this. He was right. Dancing was much better with another person.

"While we're time traveling," he said, "this would

be a good time for me to decide I want to get to know you a lot better. As I recall, we hadn't yet introduced ourselves at this point. That would be a good start. I don't believe I caught your name. I'm Ken."

"I'm Jenny."

"Nice to meet you, Jenny. I find it absolutely unbelievable that a woman as gorgeous and witty as you are is without a date, but if you don't mind, I'd like to rectify that situation. What are you doing next weekend?"

"Well, I was planning to water my plants and eat cold macaroni and cheese, but I'm open to suggestions."

"I was thinking of dinner in some place with candles on the tables, then a whole evening of slow dancing."

"I could go for that."

"Good, it's a date."

They danced a little more, then Jenny said, "Was that last bit part of the time travel—what you wished you'd said back then—or did I just accept a date for next weekend?"

"Both. If I'd been smart, that's what I would have said. But I think it would be a good start for our starting over. And I promise to warn my parents in advance so they don't show up. Are you okay with that?"

She nodded and rested her cheek against his shoulder. Then the music came to an end, and he led her back to their seats. "If we're going out next weekend, I'd better get your phone number."

"You've already got my phone number."

"Jenny, be a good sport." He pulled a pen from his shirt pocket and took a slip of paper from his jacket pocket. "Inspected by 38," he read. "I guess a phone number will fit on the back of that."

Laughing, she gave him the number, even though he'd been calling it for weeks. That was one of the many things she'd grown to love about him. He never took himself too seriously. Impulsively, she leaned forward to kiss him.

"My, aren't you the forward one," he said with a laugh when they broke off the kiss. "I normally don't kiss on the first date."

"Oh, hush," she said, kissing him again.

"We'd probably better get back to the reception before they realize we're gone," he said with a resigned sigh several minutes later.

"Do you think anyone will miss us in that crowd?"

"Sharon will miss us when they start throwing garters and bouquets."

"Then, by all means, we'd better get back."

He walked her back to the ballroom, his arm around her waist. At the doorway, she paused and looked up at him. "You know something? I'm feeling lucky tonight."

"So am I."

"And we'll know it's a miracle if I catch that bouquet."

"I've got my fingers crossed."

For the first time in all the weddings she'd gone to, Jenny actually leaped to catch the bouquet. And she became a believer in miracles.

* * * * *

Silhouette Romance is proud to present
Virgin Brides, a brand-new monthly
promotional series by some of the bestselling
and most beloved authors in the
romance genre.

In March '98, look for the very first
Virgin Brides novel,

THE PRINCESS BRIDE by Diana Palmer.

Just turn the page for an exciting preview of
Diana Palmer's thrilling new tale...

Chapter One

Tiffany saw him in the distance, riding the big black stallion. It was spring, and that meant roundup. It was not unusual to see the owner of the Lariat ranch in the saddle at dawn lending a hand to rope a stray calf or help work the branding. Kingman Marshall kept fit with ranch work, and despite the fact that he shared an office and a business partnership with Tiffany's father in land and cattle, his staff didn't see a lot of him.

This year, they were using helicopters to mass the far-flung cattle, and they had a corral set up on a wide, flat stretch of land where they could dip the cattle, check them, cut out the calves for branding and separate them from their mothers. It was physically demanding work, and no job for a tenderfoot. King wouldn't let Tiffany near it, but it wasn't a front row seat at the corral that she wanted. If she could just get his attention away from the milling cattle on the wide, rolling plain that led to the Guadalupe River, if he'd just look her way...

Tiffany stood up on a rickety lower rung of the gray

wood fence, avoiding the sticky barbed wire, and waved her Stetson at him. She was a picture of young elegance in her tan jodhpurs and sexy pink silk blouse and high black boots. She was a debutante. Her father, Harrison Blair, was King's business partner and friend, and if she chased King, her father encouraged her. It would be a marriage made in heaven. That is, if she could find some way to convince King of it. He was elusive and quite abrasively masculine. It might take more than a young lady of almost twenty-one with a sheltered, monied background to land him. But, then, Tiffany had confidence in herself; she was beautiful and intelligent.

Her long black hair hung to her waist in back, and she refused to have it cut. It suited her tall, slender figure and made an elegant frame for her soft, oval face and wide green eyes and creamy complexion. She had a sunny smile, and it never faded. Tiffany was always full of fire, burning with a love of life that her father often said had been reflected in her long-dead mother.

"King!" she called, her voice clear, and it carried in the early-morning air.

He looked toward her. Even at that distance, she could see that cold expression in his pale blue eyes, on his lean, hard face with its finely chiseled features. He was a rich man. He worked hard, and he played hard. He had women, Tiffany knew so, but he was nothing if not discreet. He was a man's man, and he lived like one. There was no playful boy in that tall, fit body. He'd grown up years ago, the boyishness driven out of him by a rich, alcoholic father who demanded blind obedience from the only child of his shallow, runaway wife.

She watched him ride toward her, easy elegance in the saddle. He reined in at the fence, smiling down at her with faint arrogance.

"You're out early, tidbit," he remarked in a deep, velvety voice with just a hint of Texas drawl.

"I'm going to be twenty-one tomorrow," she said pertly. "I'm having a big bash to celebrate, and you have to come. Black tie, and don't you dare bring anyone. You're mine, for the whole evening. It's my birthday and on my birthday I want presents—and you're it. My big present."

His dark eyebrows lifted with amused indulgence. "You might have told me sooner that I was going to be a birthday present," he said. "I have to be in Omaha early Saturday."

"You have your own plane," she reminded him. "You can fly."

"I have to sleep sometimes," he murmured.

"I wouldn't touch that line with a ten-foot pole," she drawled, peeking at him behind her long lashes. "Will you come?"

He lit a cigarette, took a long draw and blew it out with slight impatience. "Little girls and their little whims," he mused. "All right, I'll whirl you around the floor and toast your coming-of-age, but I won't stay. I can't spare the time."

"You'll work yourself to death," she complained, and then became solemn. "You're only thirty-four and you look forty."

"Times are hard, honey," he mused, smiling at the intensity in that glowering young face. "We've had low prices and drought. It's all I can do to keep my financial head above water."

"You could take the occasional break," she advised. "And I don't mean a night on the town. You could get away from it all and just rest."

"They're full up at the Home," he murmured, grinning at her exasperated look. "Honey, I can't afford vacations, not with times so hard. What are you wearing for this coming-of-age party?" he asked to divert her.

"A dream of a dress. White silk, very low in front, with diamanté straps and a white gardenia in my hair." She laughed.

He pursed his lips. He might as well humor her. "That sounds dangerous," he said softly.

"It will be," she promised, teasing him with her eyes. "You might even notice that I've grown up."

He frowned a little. That flirting wasn't new, but it was disturbing lately. He found himself avoiding little Miss Blair, without really understanding why. His body stirred even as he looked at her, and he moved restlessly in the saddle. She was years too young for him, and a virgin to boot, according to her doting, sheltering father. All those years of obsessive parental protection had led to a very immature and unavailable girl. It wouldn't do to let her too close. Not that anyone ever got close to Kingman Marshall, not even his infrequent lovers. He had good reason to keep women at a distance. His upbringing had taught him too well that women were untrustworthy and treacherous.

"What time?" he asked on a resigned note.

"About seven?"

He paused thoughtfully for a minute. "Okay." He tilted his wide-brimmed hat over his eyes. "But only for an hour or so."

"Great!"

He didn't say goodbye. Of course, he never did. He wheeled the stallion and rode off, man and horse so damn arrogant that she felt like flinging something at his tall head. He was delicious, she thought, and her body felt hot all over just looking at him. On the ground he towered over her, lean and hard-muscled and sexy as all hell. She loved watching him.

With a long, unsteady sigh, she finally turned away and remounted her mare. She wondered sometimes why she bothered hero-worshiping such a man. One of these days he'd get married and she'd just die. God forbid that he'd marry anybody but her!

That was when the first shock of reality hit her squarely between the eyes. Why, she had to ask herself, would a man like that, a mature man with all the worldly advantages, want a young and inexperienced woman like herself at his side? The question worried her so badly that she almost lost control of her mount.

The truth of her situation was unpalatable and a little frightening. She'd never even considered a life without King. What if she had to?

She rode home slowly, a little depressed because she'd had to work so hard just to get King to agree to come to her party. And still haunting her was that unpleasant speculation about a future without King...

But she perked up when she thought of the evening ahead. King didn't come to the house often, only when her father wanted to talk business away from work, or occasionally for drinks with some of her father's acquaintances. To have him come to a party was new and stimulating. Especially if it ended the way she planned. She had her sights well and truly set on the big rancher. Now all she had to do was take aim!

DIANA PALMER
ANN MAJOR
SUSAN MALLERY

MONTANA MAVERICKS Weddings

RETURN TO WHITEHORN

In April 1998 get ready to catch the bouquet. Join in the excitement as these bestselling authors lead us down the aisle with three heartwarming tales of love and matrimony in Big Sky country.

A very engaged lady is having second thoughts about her intended; a pregnant librarian is wooed by the town bad boy; a cowgirl meets up with her first love. Which Maverick will be the next one to get hitched?

Available in April 1998.

Silhouette's beloved **MONTANA MAVERICKS** returns in Special Edition and Harlequin Historicals starting in February 1998, with brand-new stories from your favorite authors.

Round up these great new stories at your favorite retail outlet.

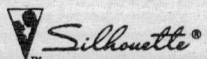

Silhouette®

Look us up on-line at: http://www.romance.net

PSMMWEDS

Take 4 bestselling love stories FREE

Plus get a FREE surprise gift!

Special Limited-time Offer

Mail to Silhouette Reader Service™

3010 Walden Avenue
P.O. Box 1867
Buffalo, N.Y. 14269-1867

YES! Please send me 4 free Silhouette Yours Truly™ novels and my free surprise gift. Then send me 4 brand-new novels every other month, which I will receive months before they appear in bookstores. Bill me at the low price of $2.90 each plus 25¢ delivery and applicable sales tax, if any.* That's the complete price and a savings of over 10% off the cover prices—quite a bargain! I understand that accepting the books and gift places me under no obligation ever to buy any books. I can always return a shipment and cancel at any time. Even if I never buy another book from Silhouette, the 4 free books and the surprise gift are mine to keep forever.

201 SEN CF2X

Name	(PLEASE PRINT)	
Address	Apt. No.	
City	State	Zip

This offer is limited to one order per household and not valid to present Silhouette Yours Truly™ subscribers. *Terms and prices are subject to change without notice. Sales tax applicable in N.Y.

USYRT-296 ©1996 Harlequin Enterprises Limited

Catch more great
HARLEQUIN™ Movies
featured on the movie channel (tmc)

Premiering March 14th
Treacherous Beauties

starring Emma Samms and Bruce Greenwood based on the novel by Cheryl Emerson

Don't miss next month's movie!
Hard to Forget
based on the novel by bestselling Harlequin Superromance® author Evelyn A. Crowe, premiering April 11th!

If you are not currently a subscriber to The Movie Channel, simply call your local cable or satellite provider for more details. Call today, and don't miss out on the romance!

the movie channel (tmc)
100% pure movies.
100% pure fun.

HARLEQUIN™
Makes any time special.™

Harlequin, Joey Device, Makes any time special and Superromance are trademarks of Harlequin Enterprises Limited. The Movie Channel is a service mark of Showtime Networks, Inc., a Viacom Company.

An Alliance Television Production

HMBPA398

BESTSELLING AUTHORS IN THE SPOTLIGHT

WE'RE SHINING THE SPOTLIGHT ON SIX OF OUR STARS!

Harlequin and Silhouette have selected stories from several of their bestselling authors to give you six sensational reads. These star-powered romances are bound to please!

THERE'S A PRICE TO PAY FOR STARDOM... AND IT'S LOW

$1.99 U.S.
$2.50 CAN.
Special Offer

As a special offer, these six outstanding books are available from Harlequin and Silhouette for only $1.99 in the U.S. and $2.50 in Canada. Watch for these titles:

At the Midnight Hour—Alicia Scott
Joshua and the Cowgirl—Sherryl Woods
Another Whirlwind Courtship—Barbara Boswell
Madeleine's Cowboy—Kristine Rolofson
Her Sister's Baby—Janice Kay Johnson
One and One Makes Three—Muriel Jensen

Available in March 1998
at your favorite retail outlet.

PBAIS

MARIE FERRARELLA's

miniseries continues with her brand-new Silhouette single title

In The Family Way

Dr. Rafe Saldana was Bedford's most popular pediatrician. And though the handsome doctor had a whole lot of love for his tiny patients, his heart wasn't open for business with women. At least, not until single mother Dana Morrow walked into his life. But Dana was about to become the newest member of the Baby of the Month Club. Was the dashing doctor ready to play daddy to her baby-to-be?

Available June 1998.

Silhouette®

Find this new title by Marie Ferrarella
at your favorite retail outlet.

Look us up on-line at: http://www.romance.net

PSMFIFWAY